Charming Sharra

The Legends of Ethshar

Charming Sharra

LAWRENCE WATT-EVANS

WILDSIDE PRESS

Dedicated to
all the readers who have kept Ethshar alive

CHAPTER ONE

Sharra stared at her husband in angry confusion, her arms folded across her chest. "What do you think you're doing?" she demanded.

He stuffed the last three tunics from the pile on the bed into the duffel. "I'm leaving," he said, as he tugged at the drawstrings. "I'll be sleeping in my shop until I can find someplace else."

"What do you mean, you're leaving?" She uncrossed her arms and shouted, "You can't leave!"

Dulzan hoisted the bag onto his shoulder. "Yes, Sharra, I can. You can have the house and everything in it—you chose it all, after all. I'll send over a share of my money, too. You can have that, but you can't have me. I am leaving you, and I hope I never see you again."

"But we're married!" she said, grabbing his arm. "You love me! You can't go!"

He shook off her hand. "We're married, yes, but I visited the magistrate this morning, and a year and a day from now we won't be. I *don't* love you—I'm not sure I ever did, but I certainly don't now. And I can do as I please, something I took much too long to realize. I am going, and I won't be back."

She stepped into the doorway, blocking his path. "I won't let you go! You're my husband, and you belong *here*."

He let out a deep sigh. "Sharra, I am leaving. I do not belong in Brightside. I was born and raised in Crafton, and I'm going home. I have had more than enough of your demands and constant quarreling, of being dragged to boring parties so you can show me off to strangers, and to your supposed friends you don't even like, and of you belittling *my* friends—who I *do* like, more than I like you. I'm tired of walking half a mile to my shop every day instead of living close by, because Crafton isn't good enough for you and you insisted we had to live here. I'm tired of *you*. After more than twenty years, I'm done. I am not going to spend the rest of my life listening to you. It's past time I gave up on the idea that you're ever going to change."

"Is there someone else?" she demanded. "Another woman? I don't mind if you want to marry someone else, I know it isn't fashionable to have multiple wives, but I'd rather have that than see you leave—I'd still be the senior even if she's the one in your bed. I could cope with it. *Please*, Dulzan!"

"There isn't anyone else, Sharra—not yet, anyway."

"Is it that Tanna? Terrek's daughter?"

"There *isn't* anyone else, Sharra!"

"But then why do you want to leave *me*?"

"For one thing, because you *won't shut up*. For another, because all you care about is what other people think of you, even though you're a terrible judge of what they *really* think, and I'm tired of it. For a third, you're constantly nitpicking, and demanding, and unhappy. When was the last time you laughed? Do you even remember *how* to laugh?"

"Of course I do! I laughed when that ninny Thed the Younger fell off the Fishertown pier!"

"He almost drowned."

"But he looked so ridiculous!"

He met her gaze for a moment, then shook his head. "Goodbye, Sharra." He pushed her aside, none too gently, and marched out of the bedroom.

She followed him down the stairs, still pleading, and out onto the front steps, but there she stopped. She did not want to let the neighbors see them fighting. She watched as Dulzan strolled down Straight South Street, looking not the least bit troubled by either the bundle on his shoulder or the fact that he was deserting his wife. In fact, there was a bounce in his step she had not seen in years, and she thought she even heard him humming.

How could he *do* this to her? Worst of all, why did he look *happy* about it?

And what was she supposed to do now? She had built her entire life around him! She had devoted herself to keeping his house spotlessly clean and tastefully decorated—and of course she had made him buy a house that was worthy of him, getting out of that run-down place in Crafton and into their lovely home here in Brightside. She had made sure all their neighbors knew that he was not just any carpenter, but a *master cabinetmaker*. She had watched to see that he only took on apprentices worthy of him—boys from good families, boys with sound teeth and good clothes, no ragged beggars from the Wall Street Field, no foul-smelling brats from Fishertown. She had not let him take on a girl, of course; who ever heard of a really good female cabinetmaker? She didn't want him to waste his time on someone who wouldn't reflect well on him. Besides, she didn't want him spending his days with a teenage girl.

He had sometimes remarked that if she really wanted his apprentices to reflect well him, she wouldn't have chosen that fumble-fingered idiot Zalmin, who didn't even *want* to be a cabinetmaker, but she had always pointed out how rich and well-connected his parents were, and that the other two she had chosen for him had turned out well. Besides, who cared what the *apprentices* wanted, so long as their parents were pleased?

Alas, she had never been able to convince him to move his *business* out of Crafton; she had explained to him that he would make more money, and attract an even better grade of apprentice, if he relocated his shop to somewhere in Brightside—perhaps Luxury Street. He had agreed that might be nice, but said that moving everything would be expensive and time-consuming, and somehow it never happened, no matter how often she reminded him. She never gave up reminding him, though, no matter how little attention he paid.

She had made sure they didn't have any children to distract her from her devotion to him; she had visited Mother Maffi, the witch in Eastside, every month without fail. She hadn't told *him* that, of course; when he brought up the subject she had always said it was just bad luck that she had never conceived. She had done *everything* for Dulzan.

And now he was gone.

But he would be back, she told herself. He would realize he couldn't get along without her. He would grow tired of a cold and lonely bed...

Unless he really *was* seeing that horrible Tanna, or some other nasty young woman.

She needed to know what he was doing down there in Crafton, Sharra told herself. If he was really sleeping alone then surely, he would come back to her! He would get lonely, and she had taken care of herself, she was still desirable.

And if he *wasn't* sleeping alone, then she wanted to know who her rival was, the better to destroy her.

Dulzan turned left onto Copper Street, out of her sight; she stared a moment longer, in hopes he would reappear, but when he did not she stormed into the house, slamming the door behind her.

She marched from room to room, straightening nicknacks and adjusting rugs, then stalked upstairs to tidy the bedroom; he had left the wardrobe standing open, and a dozen other things were out of place.

He had also left half his clothes, and the better half. The embroidered silk tunics she had bought him for Festival, one a year for each of the last eight years, were still in the wardrobe. The velvet breeches, the black suede kilt, the polished boots with silver buckles—they were all still there.

She had a moment of hope—surely, he would not have left all those expensive clothes if he really never meant to come back!

But then she realized that those were *exactly* the clothes he would have left—the ones that were too delicate for everyday use, the ones that he had not actually worn in months or years. They would be of no use in a carpentry shop. He had only worn them when he accompanied her to elegant parties, or to events at the Palace, and without her to wangle invitations, he would not be attending any more such gatherings.

He probably thought that was a *good* thing! Where would he be without her to improve his behavior?

But then she frowned. Much as she hated to admit it, he had never really *wanted* to improve himself, no matter what she had done to explain it to him. He just wanted to spend his time with his friends and family in Crafton—despite years of effort on her part, he didn't want to be part of the city's elite, chatting with lords and ladies. He just wanted to build beautiful things in that foul-smelling shop of his, and tell stupid jokes with the neighbors, and go to Tizzi's Tavern to eat their spicy fried fish, drink their strong beer, and sing bawdy songs with his friends as the beer got to him. Then, when he'd had enough, he would come home to sleep soundly before starting over again the next day, and he never seemed happy when Sharra forced him to change this routine. He didn't care that his work was so fine he could have charged the sort of prices for his cabinetry that wizards charged for spells, rather than the pittance other carpenters earned. He knew that he had furnished the overlord's own office, and he was proud of that, but he didn't want to *do* anything with it; he wouldn't advertise it to the wealthy people of Brightside. He barely spoke to them; he dismissed them as *her* friends. It drove Sharra half mad with frustration sometimes, that he didn't want to better himself.

Why would he leave her? *She* was the one who was constantly disappointed!

Why *would* he want to leave her? He said it was because she never shut up, but she had *always* been talkative. She hadn't changed. They had gotten together when she was eighteen and he was twenty-three, and she was still just the same as she had been then.

She frowned. Or was she? She closed the wardrobe and looked at herself in the mirror.

She had been quite a beauty in her day; that was why Dulzan wanted her in the first place. She was still attractive, but she had to admit she was not what she had been when they first met. Her hair was not quite as glossy, her skin not as smooth, her bosom perhaps a bit less prominent. When she frowned at her reflection it wasn't cute anymore, and there were lines at the corners of her mouth.

Maybe that was it. Maybe she wasn't pretty enough anymore. She had always known that Dulzan had married her for her looks—but then, *she* had married *him* for *his* looks. Those muscles! That smile! And even as a journeyman he had obviously been destined for success; his work had always been wonderful. That idol of Piskor the Generous that he had carved for his mother's household shrine was amazing, and only seemed to get even more beautiful with time.

Sharra had never quite completed her own apprenticeship; she had decided she would rather be Dulzan's wife than a journeyman weaver, so she had walked out of her parents' shop and never bothered with the final assessment. She had devoted herself to taking care of her husband instead, and had not touched a loom in over twenty years—but now she might need to find a way to earn her own living. He had said he would send her money, but she doubted it would be enough to live on for the rest of her life.

She stared at her reflection. Maybe if she was still young and beautiful he wouldn't have left.

Or maybe if she was young and beautiful *again*, he would come back! She frowned, then immediately caught herself—that frown made her look awful.

Youth spells were expensive. Maybe she could buy a love spell, instead. The next time she visited Eastside she would ask Mother Maffi about that.

But there were stories about love spells going wrong, and a youth spell had a certain appeal all its own—not only would she be beautiful enough to lure Dulzan back, but it would extend her own life by decades. Mortality was not exactly looming, she wasn't yet forty, but pushing the inevitable back a couple of decades might be nice.

Well, she did not need to decide immediately. After all, Dulzan might come back on his own, once he had spent a night or two alone, and had lived without anyone to pick up after him, or prepare healthy meals for him.

She would wait and see.

And if he *did* come back, she would make sure to remind him regularly how silly he had been to ever think he could live without her.

CHAPTER TWO

Dulzan did not return.

Sharra waited three days, to let him stew a little, before she even told anyone he was gone, let alone visited his shop. She spent three days visiting her friends in Brightside, browsing the stores in the Merchants' Quarter but not buying anything, and pretending everything was normal, never mentioning to anyone that Dulzan was no longer living with her. She spent three nights alone in their fine big bed, staring up at the canopy for what seemed like hours, before falling asleep.

When she did finally decide that she would need to take direct action she dressed in her best gray satin tunic and blue velvet skirt, with a fine broad-brimmed felt hat cocked over her right ear, three long feathers curling down into the silky black locks that tumbled past her shoulders. She had spent half an hour at the mirror, powdering her face and plucking a few hairs that had dared to grow where they were not wanted. She knew she did not look eighteen, but she thought she looked good. Satisfied, she marched down to the shop on Carpenter Street and swept through the shop's wide front door, ready to win Dulzan back with her charms.

The place reeked of sawdust and varnish, just as it always had—she had always avoided visiting him at work because of the smell. Dulzan was seated at the workbench in the back, singing some silly song about a fisherman and a sea-woman quietly to himself as he put the finishing touches on an elaborately-carved drawer front. He looked up at the jingle of the bell, then carefully wiped varnish from his brush with a bit of rag, and set both brush and rag aside.

"Hello, Sharra," he said cheerfully. "You look well; does single life agree with you?"

That was not the reaction she had expected, and she was completely unprepared for the question. "I miss you," she blurted out.

He shook his head. His smile vanished. "That's too bad," he said, reaching for his brush. "I don't miss *you*." He leaned over and eyed a carved blossom critically, checking to see whether every detail was evenly coated with varnish. "I thought I had made my feelings clear. They haven't changed. If you're here about the money I promised you, it's in the back—I was going to send my sister over to give it to you, but she's been busy."

"You weren't going to bring it yourself?"

He dabbed the tip of the brush between two petals of the wooden chrysanthemum, then shook his head. "No," he said. "I don't want to ever see that house again. Or you, for that matter. I said that. So you did come for the money?"

"No," Sharra said, struggling to maintain her composure. She hadn't expected him to be so cold. "I came to see *you*. I really do miss you. I want everything back the way it was."

He sighed, and straightened on his stool as he looked at her again. "That's unfortunate, because it never will be," he said. "I suggest you get over it."

"But Dulzan, I love you!"

"I doubt that. You just don't want to give up anything you think belongs to you. Well, Sharra, I *don't* belong to you. I belong to *me*."

"But I want you back!"

"You can't have me. Let me get the money, and you can take that and go. You don't belong here." He put the brush down again, slid off the stool, and headed into the back room.

"No, wait, Dulzan!" Sharra called, but he ignored her and vanished through the doorway.

She stood in the middle of the shop, casting glances in several directions—at the street outside the window, at the workbench, at the display of various woods on the far wall, at the doorway to the back room. She wanted to follow him, but if she did her velvet skirt would get sawdust on it, and velvet was so hard to clean...

And then he was back, holding out a leather pouch, a big one. "Here," he said, offering it to her.

She accepted it, and almost dropped it; it was much heavier than she had expected. Startled, she stared at it.

He returned to his stool and picked up his brush, then leaned forward to study the carving.

Sharra looked at the pouch, looked at Dulzan, then back at the pouch. Warily, she opened it, and stared at its contents.

It was full of gold. She had never seen so much gold in one place before. She had not really given much thought to Dulzan's talk about giving her money, but she had assumed it would be coppers, maybe a few bits in silver; this was *at least* a few rounds of gold.

"Where did you *get* all this?" she demanded.

"I earned it," he said, setting the brush down again without looking at her. "I think this is done." He carefully picked up the drawer and set it to one side.

"But...I had no idea you had so much!"

"Of course not," he said. "If you knew, you'd have spent it. You'd have bought me fancy clothes, and expensive dinners, and you'd have taken us to concerts and dances and I don't know what all. You'd probably have rebuilt the house, and I'd have had to live through that with you. So I hid it from you. I've been hiding it for years. I learned to do that by the time we'd been married a year."

She held out the purse. "But you just *gave* it to me!"

"Yes, and now you can go spend it on all the fancy clothes and food and jewelry and shows you want, but *I* won't have to go along. Now, go away—go spend your money."

"But what will *you* live on?"

He looked at her, then waved a hand at his surroundings. "I have all I need, Sharra, including plenty of eager customers, one of whom is due any minute now to go over some drawings for her new wardrobe. *You're* the one who has no income, which is why I gave you that. Between the house and what you have there, even with your expensive tastes, with a little care you should be fine for at least a few years, and by then I expect you'll either have a new husband or will have found some sort of work. *I* don't need it."

Just then the bell chimed behind her; Sharra turned to see a plain-looking thirtyish woman stepping into the shop. She wore a simple yellow tunic trimmed with red embroidery, and a green wool skirt. "Am I interrupting?" she asked.

"Not at all!" Dulzan said, rising from his stool. "Come in! I have the sketches ready."

The newcomer cast an uncertain glance at Sharra.

"Oh, let me introduce you," Dulzan said. "Filana, this is my former wife, Sharra the Petty. Sharra, this is Filana of Shadyside."

Sharra winced. "He's just joking," she said. "I'm called Sharra the Charming."

"It's not a joke," Dulzan said. "It's what everyone calls you, Sharra. Nobody else thinks you're charming; I haven't heard anyone else refer to you that way in a dozen years."

"Maybe I should come back…" Filana began, looking uneasily from one to the other.

"No, I'm going," Sharra said. "You go ahead with your business." She turned and strode out of the shop, the feathers on her hat brushing against the door as she went. She clutched the leather pouch in both hands as she marched up Carpenter Street, struggling not to let any tears flow down her flushed cheeks.

How could Dulzan do that to her? Calling her that horrible name in front of one of his customers, calling her his *former* wife when they were still technically married, treating her so coldly…

He wasn't coming back to her, she realized. He really wasn't. It wasn't just a matter of time. He wouldn't reconsider. He really, truly did not want her anymore.

She picked up her pace, hurrying away from the shop, until she reached the corner, where she abruptly stopped.

She needed to talk to somebody, someone she could explain everything to. She could not think of anyone among her friends and neighbors back in Brightside who she could talk to about something like this; she had spent the last three days pretending nothing was wrong, smiling when she saw them in the street, waving as if everything was fine, stopping in for tea, chatting about the weather and the latest scandal at the Palace and the newest hats for sale in the Merchants' Quarter, and whether warlocks were a danger to everyone or just another kind of magician.

She didn't have the sort of close friends she could talk to about this; she needed family, she decided. She turned around and headed back down Carpenter Street, past Dulzan's shop, where she resolutely did not look in the windows, to Weaver Street, where she turned east.

She hesitated when she reached the door of her parents' shop. She had not visited since last Festival, five months ago. The sign over the door was freshly painted – runes spelled out KIRSHA THE WEAVER, FINE FABRICS, over the outline of a loom. It was much like a dozen others on the street; her parents had always relied on word of mouth to attract business, not on fancy signs.

She decided that knocking would be silly; she was *family*, after all. She opened the door and stepped in.

Her mother was sitting behind the counter, reading a book; she looked up at the sound of the door, and almost dropped the book as her mouth fell open in surprise. "Sharra!" she exclaimed.

"Hello, Mama," Sharra said.

"What's wrong?" Kirsha asked, getting to her feet and setting the book aside.

"What makes you think anything's wrong?" Sharra asked, irritated.

"Your face! You look miserable. Besides, except for Festival you never come here unless something's wrong."

"My face? Is it really that obvious?"

"To *me* it is – I'm your mother! Now, what's wrong?"

"You haven't heard?" She knew no one in Brightside would have heard anything, but she had thought word would get around in Crafton; Dulzan had no reason to keep the news quiet.

"Oh. The rumors are true? Dulzan left you? You didn't throw him out?"

"*No*, I didn't throw him out!" she wailed. "I love him!"

Kirsha dashed out from behind the counter to wrap her daughter in a reassuring hug. "I'm sorry, sweetling. I heard stories, but I didn't know what to believe – you know how nasty some of the neighbors can be. Everyone said Dulzan was sleeping in his shop, but I didn't know how serious it was; I thought it might have been a little spat that the gossips blew up into a big fight. I thought about coming to see you, but you know I always feel out of place in Brightside."

"I know, Mama. That's all right." She pulled out of the suffocating embrace.

Kirsha grabbed Sharra's hand and dragged her through the curtain to the back room. "Sit down, sit down," she said. "Tell me about it. What happened? Why did he go? What did you fight about?"

Sharra settled onto an ancient chair, while her mother perched on a stool facing her. "There wasn't any fight," she said. "Three days ago I came home from the market and he was packing a bag, and then he just *left*. He said he would send me money and sleep in his shop and he never wanted to see me again. He said he'd reported it to the magistrate, and in a year and a day our marriage would be over."

"He just *left*? He must have said *why!*"

"He said he was tired of quarreling."

"Oh. Did you quarrel a lot?"

Sharra hesitated. "*I* didn't think so," she said. "I mean, we didn't always agree on everything, but I don't remember any *fighting*."

"*I* never heard you quarreling, exactly," Kirsha agreed. "But I didn't see you that often after you moved up to Brightside."

Sharra decided she did not want to talk about that. "Where's Papa?" she asked.

"He went up to Grandgate to buy more wool; the stockroom is almost empty."

"Is business good?"

"Oh, well," Kirsha said, turning up an empty palm. "We do all right. It would be easier with more hands; Kelder and I aren't as young as we used to be."

"You don't have any apprentices?"

"Not at the moment, no." She sighed. "To be honest, Sharra, I don't think anyone wants to apprentice their kids to us anymore."

"What about Dallisa's kids?"

Kirsha cocked her head at her daughter. "Sharra, three of our grandchildren *did* apprentice with us, Dallisa's Arris and Lador, and Nerra's Thetheran – you must have known that. But they're all journeymen now! Arris will probably be a master in her own right soon. And they've all gone off to work elsewhere, though I'm hoping Arris will come back." She looked accusingly at her youngest daughter. "*You* didn't have any children to help out!"

"I didn't... Dulzan..." Sharra stopped, unsure what to say. *Dulzan* had wanted children, but she hadn't. She hadn't wanted to have her life turned upside-down by a baby.

"Oh, don't worry about it," her mother said, waving a hand in dismissal. "It didn't happen." Then her expression changed. "Is that why Dulzan left? To find a younger wife who will bear him children?"

"I don't *know*," Sharra admitted. "It might be. He says there isn't another woman, but I don't know."

"If you'd had children, maybe you wouldn't have nagged him so much."

"I didn't…!" Then she stopped. Maybe she *had* nagged Dulzan a little. He had said she never shut up, and most of what she had talked to him about was ways he could do better. She hadn't thought of it as nagging, but…

"You nagged him, Sharra," Kirsha said gently. "Maybe you didn't quarrel, but you nagged. When we saw you at Festival you were always nagging him to do more, to drink less, to talk to more important people. Even when you were young, before you were even *married*, you were always picking at him, telling him what to do. To be honest, I thought he *liked* it, he put up with so much. I thought he must just want to hear your voice, and never cared what you were saying. I never saw him argue with you – did you save your fights until you got home?"

"We never *had* any fights!"

Kirsha's disbelief was plain on her face. "The way you bossed him around?"

"We *didn't*! I swear! When he got mad at me he would just go down to his shop and work until his temper improved. He never even shouted at me."

"In twenty years of marriage he never yelled at you? Never… never hit you?"

"No! We loved each other!" She paused. "Or I thought we did." She remembered just how *often* he had gone to his shop to let his temper cool.

"By the gods, Sharra! No wonder he left."

"What?" Sharra stared at her mother, seriously confused.

"The way you treated him? And he *never* fought back? Of course he's gone!"

"But… No, it wasn't like that! He didn't… *I* didn't…"

"Did you treat him at home the same way you treated him in public?"

"I…sometimes…"

Kirsha shook her head. "Sharra, if you treat a man like that, sooner or later he won't take any more. You're lucky Dulzan just left peacefully, and didn't beat you first. If he ever *had* lost his temper –

well, if he'd done it a long time ago maybe you could have worked things out, but after twenty years..."

"He should have *told* me if it bothered him! He never said anything!"

Kirsha opened her mouth to say something, then thought better of it. She sighed.

"If he was so unhappy, why didn't he *tell* me?" Sharra demanded.

"Are you sure he *didn't*? Did you ever listen?"

"Of course I listened!" Sharra said, jumping to her feet. "Why are you on *his* side?"

"I'm just..."

"Mama, I'm not a child! I know what's going on; he just doesn't want me anymore because I'm getting old."

"I don't think..." Kirsha began.

Sharra did not wait to hear what her mother didn't think. "We'll just see about that!" she said, charging out the door.

She marched along Weaver Street, then turned onto Carpenter and headed north. She could see three or four people in Dulzan's shop, so she did not stop in; she kept going, the heavy purse in her hand.

He had never complained about her nagging. He had never argued with her. When she had said they should do something, he had always gone along. Oh, when they were young and foolish, sometimes he would say he didn't want to go to parties and receptions and concerts, but he had always given in eventually. He had not really protested in *years*. He had always gone, even if he did not seem to enjoy them. That wasn't it, she was *sure* that wasn't it.

No, it was because she was no longer the young beauty he had been smitten with – but with all that gold, she could *be* that girl again. If cosmetics and fine clothes weren't enough, she could buy a youth spell.

Or she could use a love spell, or some other magic. She would make him come back somehow, she told herself as she strode home. No matter what it took, she would get him back. Everything would be the way it was before!

CHAPTER THREE

The witch in Eastside called herself Mother Maffi, but Sharra doubted it was her real name. Didn't true names have magical power? Whatever her real name, she had a little shop on Smallgate Street, between Blue Road and Halfway Street, that smelled of flowers and ginger. The signboard over the front door said simply "Witch" – apparently, like Sharra's parents, she relied on word of mouth, not any sort of advertising. Sharra had found her long ago through a referral from an old friend, Desset of Carder Street.

It occurred to Sharra as she marched up Smallgate Street that she had not heard from Desset for quite some time – years, in fact. She wondered why, then realized that the last time she had seen Desset, Desset had been seven months pregnant, and Sharra had been...well, not kind about her appearance and probable future.

But surely Desset wouldn't have let that end their friendship! Perhaps, once she had Dulzan back, and things were back the way they had been, she would find Desset and see how she was doing. She was probably still living on Southeast Street.

Mother Maffi looked up from her knitting as Sharra stepped into the shop. "Oh, hello," the witch said, lowering the needles. "I didn't expect you for another sixnight."

"This is something different," Sharra said. "I think I need a love spell." She did not think witches did youth spells, and a love spell might be even better.

The witch cocked her head and set her knitting to one side, on the shelf in front of her little shrine to Bellab. "I thought you were married," she said.

"I was," Sharra said. "I am. But my husband..." She took a deep breath. "He left me. I want him back. I want everything back the way it was. I need a love spell."

Maffi frowned. "I don't do love spells," she replied. "No respectable witch does. They're dangerous and unreliable, when they work at all."

"But I thought – "

"No love spells," Maffi said, in a tone that brooked no argument.

Sharra looked at her pleadingly. "You're *sure* you can't make an exception?"

"I can't, and I won't. Why did your man leave? Was he seeing someone else?"

"He says he wasn't, but he's not seeing *me*," Sharra snapped.

Maffi grimaced. "Oh. Perhaps I can help somehow? Not with a love spell – to be honest, I wouldn't even know how to attempt one. But I know some herbs that can be useful if a marriage has cooled off."

Sharra shook her head. "That's not what I need. So witches don't do love spells?"

"No, we don't."

"Who does? Wizards? Sorcerers? Theurgists?"

"I've heard some wizards can."

"Can you tell me where to find one of them?"

Maffi tapped her chin thoughtfully. "You know Wizard Street is just a block north, don't you? There are wizards living and working on the other side of the courtyard behind this house. I've spoken with several of them when we're out fetching water or doing laundry or dumping slops."

"Does one of them do love spells? Or youth spells?"

"Youth spells?"

"Love spells or youth spells, yes."

"Well, which do you want?"

"Why? Can *you* make me young again?"

Maffi smiled wryly. "Would I look like this if I could? I can do some healing and slow aging down a little, but I can't make you young again."

"Who can?"

"Well, I don't know anything about love spells, but I know a youth spell is major magic, not something anyone does lightly. If it were easy, we wouldn't have so many white-haired wizards, would we? If you want it done right, you want the most powerful wizard you can find. From what the neighbors say, the most powerful wizard right around here is Poldrian of Morningside. Go north a block on Blue Road, turn left, and his shop is two blocks up on the right."

"You know him?"

"Only by reputation. We've never met. But if it doesn't work out, he can probably recommend someone else; there are plenty of shops on Wizard Street."

"Good. Thank you." She turned and marched out without another word, letting the door close behind her.

Mother Maffi watched her go, then sighed and picked up her knitting again. Sharra had not offered to pay anything for her advice, of course.

She had known Sharra the Petty for twenty years, and she was fairly sure this was not going to end well, but she also knew Sharra wouldn't listen to a warning. She cast off the yarn, and started a new row.

She wondered whether Poldrian might pay a referral fee.

* * *

Sharra had no trouble finding the wizard's shop. His signboard did not mention his trade, but only his name – Poldrian of Morningside – but the sparkling multicolored lanterns on either side of the door, ablaze with what was obviously not any sort of natural light, made it clear the proprietor was a magician of some sort.

It was a fairly large shopfront, and beautifully finished, with polished stone and ornate shutters; the lintel above the door was carved with a pair of eyes that stared down at anyone entering. Sharra was not sure whether they actually moved as she approached, or whether that was merely an artist's trick of some sort.

The door opened silently the instant she touched the handle, but Sharra refused to be impressed or surprised; she strode into the shop and found a spacious sitting room, far larger and more elegant than Mother Maffi's little parlor, with a podium in one corner and a girl in her early teens sitting on a stool behind it, engrossed in something Sharra could not see. The girl wore an apprentice's robe, but one of fine white linen trimmed with blue silk rather than the usual plain gray fabric. A blue silk ribbon held her black hair back.

"I'm here to see the wizard," Sharra announced.

The girl looked up, and put down whatever it was she had held. "Do you have an appointment?" she asked, trying to sound grown-up but not quite managing it.

"I don't need one," Sharra said. "I'm a paying customer."

The girl blinked, then nodded. "Of course. It's usually a good idea to make an appointment, though; sometimes my master is in the middle of a spell and can't be interrupted." She slid off her stool and stood up. "I'll see if he's available. Who shall I say is here?"

"Sharra the Charming."

"Very good." The girl vanished through a door at the back of the shop.

Sharra stood in the middle of the room, waiting. She glanced around at the half-dozen chairs and the two settees, but did not consider sitting down; she was here on business, not a friendly visit. She noticed that the upholstery all looked new; it probably had a preservation spell on it. The room smelled faintly of something Sharra couldn't place, a sharp, pleasant scent that reminded her of cats.

After what seemed an unreasonably long time the girl reappeared and said, "Master Poldrian will be right out. Please make yourself comfortable."

Sharra frowned and stayed where she was as the girl resumed her place on the stool behind the podium and picked up what appeared to be a small book.

"Right out" turned out to be long enough for Sharra's impatience to grow into annoyance verging on anger; she was tapping her foot by the time Poldrian appeared.

The wizard was a man of medium height and indeterminate age, his hair worn unusually long and his beard trimmed to a point. He wore an ankle-length black robe and a flat black cap, and he appeared not by walking through the door as the girl had, but by stepping out of thin air a few feet in front of his customer. "Yes?" he said.

This sudden magical manifestation startled and even impressed Sharra, but she was not about to admit that. "I'm here for a spell," she said.

"I perform spells," the wizard said dryly. "Many spells. You'll need to be more specific."

Sharra's patience had worn very thin by this point, so she got straight to the point. "My husband left me," she said. "I want him back."

"Ah. You want a love spell?"

Sharra nodded. She was going to add, "or a youth spell," but the wizard continued before she could speak.

"Well, I know half a dozen love spells, but the exact effects vary, and may not be appropriate for your situation. Sit down, and we can discuss it." He gestured at one of the chairs.

Sharra hesitated. She was not accustomed to sitting down when dealing with tradesmen and shopkeepers. She expected to tell them what she wanted, and have them fetch it for her. She had not usually sat down when she visited Mother Maffi.

There were exceptions, though, such as hairdressers, and she supposed wizards might reasonably be another. She settled reluctantly onto a green velvet chair.

Poldrian sat on a matching chair and said, "Tell me what happened."

"I came home one day and found him packing, and then he just left!" Sharra exclaimed. "I waited, I thought he would come to his senses or get lonely, but he hasn't come back. I want to bring him home to me! I want everything back the way it was!"

Poldrian nodded thoughtfully. "Did he say *why* he left?"

"He said I nagged and argued too much!"

Poldrian started to say something, then apparently thought better of it. "I see," he said instead.

Sharra suspected that he had wanted to ask, "*Did* you nag and argue too much?" but had thought better of antagonizing a customer. She ignored that suspicion and continued.

"I want a spell that will make him want me the way he did when we were young, so he'll come back to me and *stay*, and we can go on the way we were. I want everything back the way it was."

"Ah. Well, let's see. The Spell of Aroused Lust would not be suitable, as it wears off after a few days, and it really doesn't sound as if its effects are what you want. Fendel's Infatuous Love Spell might do, but it's tricky – the spell must be cast upon a sleeping subject, and you must be absolutely certain that *you* are the first living thing he sees when he awakens. There have been embarrassing incidents where the user stepped away for just a few seconds, only to find when he or she returned that the target was now madly in love with a neighbor who passed by the window, or a cat, or even a houseplant. Not to mention that should the spell ever be broken, the subject is usually very annoyed about it."

"But it would make him love me again?"

"Oh, the strength of the spell will vary from one individual to another, but in most cases he would be absolutely *devoted* to you. Obsessed with you, in fact. I was coming to that. He would probably be insanely jealous if you showed even the slightest interest in another person. He might neglect his business, as well – if he reacted strongly to the spell he would no longer worry about anything but pleasing and possessing you. You might even need to remind him to attend to basic needs such as food and sleep. It's very rare that anyone actually keeps Fendel's Infatuous Love Spell in place for more than a few sixnights, because it's exhausting dealing with that sort of attention."

Sharra frowned. "That does not…" she began.

"There are others," Poldrian interrupted. "The Infallible Love Philtre, for example, is far more benign and can't go wrong as easily. It's somewhat harder to apply, though – you must get him to drink a moderate amount of it, the exact quantity depending on his size, and it tastes absolutely horrible. It also requires several ounces of your own blood, but should a single drop of anyone else's blood be added after the preparation is complete, the spell will redirect its effects from you to whoever provided that last drop."

"But it works? And it doesn't turn him into someone else the way that other one did?"

"It works, and the result is much milder than the Infatuous Love Spell, though there may still be some minor personality changes – after all, he'll be in love with you, and he isn't now, so *something* must change. But he won't be obsessed to the point he might starve himself." The wizard hesitated. "I must mention one other drawback, though. The counter-spell for the Infatuous Love Spell is very simple and inexpensive; the counter for the Infallible Philtre is extremely difficult to obtain, and therefore costs far more than the original spell. Also, it might take years to acquire – it isn't something anyone keeps in stock. If you ever came to regret using the spell, breaking it might be quite a challenge."

Curious, Sharra asked, "What is it that's so hard to get?"

"The blood of a particular sort of dragon."

"I thought every wizard kept dragon's blood on hand."

"We do – but not *that* kind. As I said, it's a particular *sort* of dragon, and not one that's easy to find. It's really only useful as a counter-charm for a few rarely-used spells, and the Infallible Love

Philtre is the only one I know of that doesn't have another, easier counter, so there isn't much need for it." He appeared to consider for a moment, then said, "There are other options. Cauthen's Remarkable Love Spell is very similar in its effects, but somewhat more difficult to perform; for that one you would need some of your husband's hair or a vial of his perspiration, and *you* would need to drink the potion. The resulting love is perhaps somewhat milder than the Infallible Love Philtre, and *far* less extreme than the Infatuous Love Spell. There are two possible counter-spells – that same dragon's blood as the Philtre, or a decoction of virgin's blood taken over four nights. That might be your best option."

The thought of drinking a nasty potion was unappealing. "Are there others?"

"Oh, yes. Those are merely the easiest, and therefore the least expensive. Galger's Aphrodisiac is not much more difficult than Cauthen's, but I don't think it's what you're after – it doesn't so much cause anyone to fall in love as to provoke uncontrollable lust under certain circumstances. That can prove embarrassing should the spell be triggered in public. Fendel's Aphrodisiac Philtre is a little more flexible, but it isn't really much better if you're after a normal marital relationship. Now, the Spell of Enthrallment…but no, I don't think that would really suit your situation. It isn't permanent, and it induces obedience, not really love." He frowned. "I believe that's all the love spells I know at present, though I might be able to find more, for a suitable price."

"I…" She was unsure what to say. None of those really sounded entirely satisfactory.

"I really think that Cauthen's would be your best choice. Of course, it's not cheap."

Sharra was having second thoughts about trying a love spell. She wanted Dulzan back, but she didn't want to *change* him; she just wanted everything back the way it was before he left. And she didn't like the idea of drinking some horrible potion made with hair and sweat, let alone trying to get those things from Dulzan. Her earlier idea of restoring her former beauty still seemed like the best option. "What about youth spells?" she said.

Poldrian blinked. "That's rather different. I thought you wanted your husband back."

"I do! And I'm sure that if I was still the young beauty he married, he'd come back. I've just aged so much in twenty years!"

Poldrian considered her face, then said, "You are still quite attractive, my dear."

"But nothing like what I was as a girl! What youth spells do you know?"

"Well, the classic is Enral's Eternal Youth, but I really don't think I'm up to that – you'd need to find a more skilled wizard than I, and the cost is prohibitive for most people. What's more, it's one of the handful of regulated spells; casting it on anyone other than a wizard needs to be approved by the Wizards' Guild, and I doubt very much they would approve anything so frivolous as wanting to lure back your husband. Also, you don't need to *stay* young forever, do you? You just want to be twenty years younger, and then age normally."

Sharra hesitated, then nodded. "That's right."

"Maybe I could use Fendel's Greater Transformation to do it, but for that it would help if I had an image of your younger self. Or perhaps Javan's Restorative might work, though I've never heard of anyone using it as a youth spell – adjusted properly it would restore you to perfect health, and that might make you look younger. But I think the obvious solution is probably the best: Hallin's Bath of Youth and Vigor."

"How does that work?"

"It's simple enough from the subject's point of view, though it's quite difficult to perform. It isn't well known at all; I doubt there are a dozen wizards in all of Ethshar who can do it. In fact, I've only ever done it once before, so I'll need some time to refresh my memory and get everything ready. The basic procedure is this: I will prepare a bath, you will soak in it, and every hour you soak will subtract roughly a year from your age."

"That sounds perfect!"

"If you just want to restore your youth, then yes, it should serve. It isn't a love spell, though; once it's done it will still be up to you to get your husband back. Furthermore, be aware that there *is* no known counter-spell; if there's any way to reverse its effects, I've never heard of it, and I always research the counters for all my spells. If you change your mind and wish to look your true age again, rather than like a mere girl, there is no straightforward way to undo the spell. You would need to purchase a transformation of some sort, and even then you might not be restored to your present appearance, but only to an approximation."

"Why would I ever want to change back?" Sharra asked warily. "Does it do something to my mind? Erase my memories, maybe?"

"No, no, nothing like that. I think you may have forgotten, though, how often people do not take young women seriously."

Sharra raised her chin. "They'll take *me* seriously, no matter what I look like!"

The wizard turned up an empty palm. "And then, of course, there is the cost."

Sharra's chin came down and she glowered at Poldrian. "How much does it cost, then?"

He told her. Seventy-five rounds of gold.

She blanched. Just a few days ago that would have been an unthinkable amount, but now, with that fat purse... She did a quick calculation. Her entire supply of cash, including everything Dulzan had given her, would cover almost half of it – or really, to be honest, about two-fifths. She could sell the house in Brightside – much as she loved it, if giving it up meant she got Dulzan back, it would be worth it. She knew she could not get a good price on short notice, but she still thought that should bring another thirty rounds or so, after everything. Once she and Dulzan were together again they could buy another house, perhaps in an even better neighborhood; he must have plenty of money hidden away somewhere, or he wouldn't have given her so much.

"Perhaps I could pay half now, and the rest when my husband comes back to me?"

Poldrian had started to turn away; now he turned back. He looked surprised.

"I said seventy-five rounds *of gold.*"

"Yes, I heard you. I can't pay it all right now, but I'm sure I can manage it eventually."

Poldrian stared at her for a moment, then said, "It's customary to pay the full amount as soon as the spell is complete."

"But I don't have that much right now!"

Poldrian sighed. "Then you'll just have to get it, or stay your true age." He started to turn away again."

"No, wait!" Sharra struggled to think, to get words out. "I can... I can pay two-thirds now. That's really all I have." It was, in truth, *more* than she had; it assumed selling the house for a decent price. "But I'll get the rest in a sixnight once the spell is done, and I get my husband back."

Poldrian considered her, studying her face. At first Sharra thought he was trying to decide whether she looked honest, but then she realized he was probably trying to judge what she had looked like twenty years ago, to see whether she really would be beautiful enough to win Dulzan back.

She gazed back, forcing a small smile and trying to look charming.

"You're *sure* you can pay the rest?"

"Yes! Yes, completely."

"You're sure you want to do this, even at that price?"

"Yes!"

He was silent for another long moment. Then at last he sighed, and said, "You know there are dire penalties for failing to pay a wizard's bill?"

"I've heard that, yes." She had not actually heard it, but it was hardly surprising.

"It's the truth. If you don't pay me, I promise you, you'll regret it. You'll need to sign a contract agreeing to accept whatever penalty I choose."

"I said I'll pay you!" She tried not to sound desperate.

"Then bring the money you have four days from now, and perhaps a few favorite foods, maybe a book, or something to keep your hands busy – after all, you'll be spending twenty hours in a bathtub. You can't take any breaks. Once you get out of the bath the spell is done; you can't get back in. The magic breaks down the instant it's no longer touching you."

"Four days." She nodded.

"I'll expect you around midday."

Sharra smiled. Four days was longer than she wanted to wait, but it wasn't *too* bad, and it would give her time to raise as much of the money as she could. She was fairly sure she could sell the house in four days if she took a low enough price. She could wait four days if it meant going back to her comfortable old life with Dulzan, and having everything back the way it was before – well, everything except the house.

"I'll be here," she said.

CHARMING SHARRA | 29

CHAPTER FOUR

Four days later Sharra walked into Poldrian's shop with a heavy bag under her arm. "I'm here," she said.

Poldrian's apprentice, behind the podium, looked up from whatever she was reading. "Sharra? That's your name, isn't it? I'll tell my master you've arrived."

The wait was much shorter this time; Poldrian appeared within a few minutes, not by magically stepping out of nowhere but simply by walking out the door at the back of the parlor. The apprentice followed him and resumed her place at the podium.

"So you've come," the wizard said.

"Of course I did!" Sharra replied.

"I thought you might have reconsidered."

"Why would I do that?" Sharra demanded. "I want my husband back! I want to be young and beautiful again!"

"Yes, you said you'd be back, but I wasn't convinced you could raise the money."

Sharra pursed her lips. "I have it here." She hoisted her bag. "Fifty rounds of gold."

"The price is seventy-five."

"This is the first payment, as we agreed."

He looked at it unhappily. "The first payment? Not the whole thing?"

"This is all I have!" Sharra shouted. "It's *fifty rounds of gold*! I *told* you I can't pay it all in advance. Who has that much money on hand?"

Poldrian sighed. "And what about the rest?"

"I'll have it in a sixnight. My husband will pay it, once I've seduced him again."

"Are you *sure* of that?" Poldrian frowned at her. "There is still time to change your mind. And I'll warn you right now, I'll give you two sixnights after the spell is complete, no more, and if you haven't paid by then I'll have to do something drastic. I can't let anyone think I give discounts because someone has a good story."

Sharra had absolutely no doubt she could get the rest of the money, but she was curious – and perhaps just a *little* concerned. Things can go wrong. "What *sort* of something drastic? Kill me? Won't the magistrates get upset?"

"No, I'm not going to just kill you. I can't collect what I'm owed from a corpse, and as you say, the magistrate wouldn't like it. Even wizards can only go so far."

"What, then?"

Poldrian sighed, and shook his head. "*I* don't know. I haven't decided for certain. Turn you to stone, maybe, and tell your friends and family you'll stay that way until they pay me what I'm owed."

Sharra cocked her head. "You can do that? And turn me back?"

"Of course I can! And I've been meaning to try out a petrifaction spell I found that I've never used – I was thinking I might try it on a stray cat, but if you volunteer…" He shook his head. "But I would much rather you pay me on time."

"I will! You'll get your money!" Sharra snapped.

"You're sure?"

"I'm sure! Dulzan will pay you, if I can't!"

"And if this Dulzan gets eaten by a dragon?"

"Then my mother will pay it! Or somebody will. I have friends, wizard, friends and family. Now, can we get on with it?"

Poldrian turned up a hand, clearly unhappy but not willing to abandon the project. He signaled to the girl at the podium, who pulled a roll of parchment from somewhere. "Give my apprentice the money, and sign the contract."

Sharra obeyed, setting the heavy bag on the podium with a thump and a snort, and accepting the parchment in exchange. She unrolled it and glanced at it, saw that it seemed straightforward – she would be made physically twenty years younger, in exchange for seventy-five rounds of coined gold, paid in full by the eighth of Harvest, YS 5208. If the spell did not work as promised, all her money would be refunded except one round to defray the cost of materials. If she failed to pay in full on time, Poldrian would be free to inflict any non-fatal and at least theoretically reversible penalty he chose.

"Count the money," Poldrian instructed the apprentice.

"I don't…" Sharra began, looking up from the contract, clearly offended.

"Silence!" the wizard thundered, and Sharra fell silent. She snatched up the pen that lay on the podium and dashed off her signature at the bottom of the contract.

The apprentice quickly stacked the big gold coins on the podium, ten to each stack, then announced, "It's all here. Fifty rounds."

"Good," Poldrian said, as Sharra glared. The wizard beckoned to her. "This way," he said.

Sharra followed him into the back, but instead of along the corridor or into a workshop as she had expected, Poldrian led her around a corner and down a stairway into a windowless stone room.

Most houses in Ethshar of the Sands did not have basements; the soft soil was sufficiently unstable to make them difficult to build and maintain, and the water table high enough to make them prone to flooding. Poldrian had apparently installed one anyway. The walls were some rough-hewn gray stone, and the floor was slate – obviously either imported from somewhere or conjured up, since there was no slate to be found anywhere near the city. Four oil lamps provided some light, but the room was still very dim compared to the bright daylight above.

The room was perhaps twenty feet square, and mostly empty, but a large copper tub stood in the center. Sharra hesitated at the sight of it.

"I made most of the preparations already," Poldrian said, crossing to a large cabinet on the far side of the room. "It took hours, and I didn't want to keep you waiting around that long – especially since I couldn't be sure it would work on the first try. The magic is surprisingly stable, though, so if you hadn't come I'm sure I'd have found a use for it eventually. Perhaps I would have used it on myself." He opened the cabinet to reveal several shelves of large earthenware jugs. He took one of them from the top row and carried it to the waiting tub, then pulled the stopper and began pouring.

Sharra had expected water, but instead saw silvery liquid pour from the jug, not quite like anything she had ever seen before. It seemed to shine in the dim lamplight, and a strange scent, a little like the air before a thunderstorm, reached her.

He paused, the jug still at least half full. "This is your last chance to change your mind and save your money. If you have fifty rounds of gold, do you really need a man who preferred to leave you?"

"I want my husband back!" Sharra exclaimed. "I want everything back the way it was, and if it costs me all the money in the World, I don't care!"

"You don't *have* all the money in the World, remember. You still need another twenty-five rounds."

"You'll get your money!"

"Then you're sure you want to continue?"

"Of course I'm sure!"

Poldrian shook his head, then resumed pouring.

When the first jug was empty the wizard returned to the cabinet and fetched the next. He made several trips, pouring jug after jug into the copper tub, and placing each empty container on the floor beside the cabinet. He ignored his waiting customer throughout this process; he had offered her a last chance.

Sharra wondered why he didn't have some magical servant, or at least his apprentice, handle this task. Perhaps the spell required the wizard do it himself. She looked more closely and saw his lips moving; perhaps he was reciting an incantation.

At last the tub was almost full, and all the jugs were empty and lined up along the wall. Satisfied, Poldrian turned to Sharra and said, "Now, if you will remove your clothing and step into the tub, the spell will begin."

"Remove my clothing?" Sharra turned to glare at him.

"Well, yes. You can't take anything into the bath with you; it would be ruined, and depending on its composition it might be dangerous."

Sharra frowned. She had not expected this, but she had to admit it made some sense. "Turn away," she said.

Poldrian started to say something, then thought better of it. He turned his back on his annoying customer and waited until he heard splashing, and then heard the splashing stop. He turned back.

Sharra was sitting in the tub, looking uncomfortable. She was bent down, her back arched so that the liquid covered her from the shoulders down. Her clothes were folded on the floor beside the tub.

"Don't sit hunched over like that," Poldrian told her. "Lie back. Relax. Get your hair wet. In fact, it would help if you got your face wet, as well."

"I don't…" She did not finish the sentence, but just looked down at the strange liquid. It felt odd on her skin, as if it was not wet at all, but *drying* her, and that sharp smell was much stronger now.

"If you want to complete the spell, you must do as I say," the wizard said sternly.

Reluctantly, Sharra leaned her head back against the side of the tub and stretched her legs out, heels bumping against copper. She closed her eyes.

The liquid did not *feel* like liquid. It felt like a…a motionless wind, if such a thing were possible. And the smell had something minty about it, as well as that impending-storm quality.

The wizard chanted something that hardly sounded like a human language at all, much more loudly and clearly than the muttering he had been doing while filling the tub. Sharra also heard odd little noises, clicks and thumps and splashes, but then they stopped, and the liquid began to churn gently around her, which felt as if smooth cloth was brushing lightly against her all over. She tried to relax and enjoy it, but all in all it was not a pleasant sensation.

After a moment she opened her eyes and looked up at the ceiling beams. "How long do I need to stay in this stuff?" she asked.

"Twenty hours," the wizard replied. "The spell is fully active now, and if you leave the tub before it's complete I can guarantee neither the results nor your safety."

"Twenty hours," she repeated. "That's a long time."

"You're free to sleep whenever you choose, or eat – did you bring food, as I suggested? I can even bring you a book to read, if you allow me time to place a protective spell on it first."

"I brought food," she said, sitting up and looking at Poldrian. "It's in my bag."

"I'll put it where you can reach it. A book?"

Sharra snorted derisively. "I'm not a scholar," she said. "I don't read books. What about a chamber pot?"

"You won't need one."

"In *twenty hours*? I don't know about you, wizard – "

"It's part of the magic," he said, interrupting her. "You won't need it, I promise."

Sharra hoped he was right; she did not like the idea of staying in the tub if he was wrong. Annoyed, she lay back down, trying to ignore the liquid's constant churning.

She heard footsteps departing, and when she looked up again, the wizard was gone. She hesitated, then reached for her bag and the cakes and fruit she had packed.

She had finished all the food within an hour. The boredom seemed completely unbearable, but she forced herself to tolerate it. She slept as much as she could, and woke with no idea how long it had been. She tried to distract herself by thinking about what she would do when Dulzan came crawling back to her, desperate to get into her bed again. She would hold back at first, let him beg a little, but then she would take him back, and they would buy a bigger house in Morningside, just across from the Palace. She would insist he talk to the overlord about redecorating the entire Palace. Everyone would marvel at his work, and at how fortunate he was to have such a clever and beautiful wife.

After a time, though, even these glorious fantasies began to pall. She felt as if she had been sitting in this infernal tub, feeling the magical liquid swirling and pulling at her, for months – though she still felt dry.

She had not seen the wizard since she began eating. She wondered where he was, and when he would return, and how long she had been soaking. She wished he had left a mirror, so she could check on any change in her appearance.

She began to wonder just what would happen if she climbed out of the tub. Would it really ruin the spell? Most magic happened almost instantaneously; why did *this* spell take so long? Or was the wizard playing a trick on her? He did seem to have taken a dislike to her, as so many arrogant men did; she supposed it was because they saw her strength and independence as a challenge to their authority. She put a hand on the tub's rim.

But she had paid so very much for this spell, almost everything she had – how could she risk disrupting it? And she really did not know how long it had been; she might only need another few minutes.

Or she might already have been in here for twenty hours, or even more – suppose the wizard had forgotten about her? Or what if one of his spells had gone wrong, and killed him, or turned him into a tree squid or something?

"*Hai!*" she called. "Is anyone there?"

There was no answer. The silvery-white liquid continued to bubble and swirl.

"How long have I been in here?" she demanded. "I'm getting hungry; can someone bring me more food?"

She shifted her position, waiting for a reply, but none came.

She frowned, and sat up, just as one of the oil lamps flickered and went out.

She did not like *that*. It was bad enough sitting in this stuff in the dim lamplight, but sitting down here in the dark – *that* would be unbearable.

"*What's going on?*" she shouted as loudly as she could.

The liquid whirled about her, and seemed to be speeding up. There had been bubbles all along, but now they seemed to be larger and more numerous.

Then she heard footsteps, and the wizard reappeared at the foot of the stairs. He looked at her, and noticed the more vigorous activity in the tub.

"Ah," he said. "I think it may be done soon."

"The lamp went out," Sharra said, pointing.

The wizard barely glanced at it. "It must have run out of oil," he said. "I'll have my apprentice refill it when she's finished her breakfast."

"It's not magic?" Sharra asked.

"No, it's not magic," Poldrian replied. "It's just a lamp."

"How long have I been in here?"

"Oh, I don't know. You started around midday, correct?"

"Yes!"

"Well, it's morning. You're almost done. How do you feel?"

"I don't…" Sharra stopped, and considered the question.

She was desperately bored, eager to be anywhere except this copper tub, but in fact, she felt good otherwise. She wasn't especially hungry, despite how long it had been since she ate, and as the wizard had predicted she felt no need of a privy or chamberpot. Her skin was not wrinkled, despite soaking overnight, and she was not stiff or sore anywhere, despite the lack of any padding.

"I feel good," she admitted. "But I'm *bored*."

"It won't be much longer. I put a secondary spell on the tub's contents from upstairs last night, to make sure it didn't take you back too far and turn you into a child; it will stop the magic at twenty years, no more. From the activity in the fluid, I'd say you're getting very close."

"Why is it getting so bubbly?"

"Well, you're back to an age when you were still growing; that means there's more change required, and the magic must be more energetic."

"I wasn't still growing when I was eighteen! You're going too far!"

"Oh, I doubt that. I'm sure you had reached your adult height, but most people are still filling out at that age – bones thickening, muscles growing, that sort of thing."

"I don't…" She was interrupted by a loud crack; the copper tub had split open at the end, right between her feet. The silvery fluid began spilling out, but never touched the floor; instead as soon as it emerged from the copper it turned to vapor and quickly dissipated. The liquid remaining in the tub began to evaporate, as well. In a matter of seconds Sharra was sitting naked in an empty tub.

"That's the secondary spell," Poldrian said.

Sharra clutched her arms around herself and shrieked, "Get me a towel!"

"What for?" the wizard asked. "You're perfectly dry."

"To…to cover myself!"

"Your clothes are right there," Poldrian said. "I'll look away." He turned, suiting his actions to his words.

Spitting with fury, Sharra stepped out of the ruined, empty tub and began dressing. The wizard was absolutely right; she was not wet at all.

But she was *hungry*, she realized, and *now* she needed a chamberpot. And her clothes did not feel quite right. She looked down at herself.

A lock of long black hair slipped past her shoulder and hung down where she could see it. It was glossier than her hair had been the day before, and the breast it draped across was…not bigger, but higher.

She had never consciously noticed any changes in her hair or bosom, but having twenty years reversed in a single day and night made a visible difference.

"Oh," she said. She looked up at the wizard. "I'm hungry," she said. "And I need a privy." She looked down again.

"And a mirror," she said.

CHAPTER FIVE

The wizard's apprentice directed her to the privy behind the house, then went to fetch her a slab of bread, a mug of watered wine, and a fine silvered glass. While she waited in the parlor for the food Sharra studied her hands, arms, legs, and feet.

At thirty-eight she was not an old woman, by any means, and her skin had not been spotted or wrinkled, but now it practically glowed with health and vitality. Her hair was longer and fuller, and kept falling in her way.

When the apprentice finally delivered the promised items Sharra snatched the mirror from her hands and stared into it.

The face that looked back at her was familiar, certainly, but it was not the face she was accustomed to seeing. It was how she had always pictured herself, yes; it was a face remembered in her dreams, both waking and sleeping. It was not, however, the face she had seen every day in recent years.

It was the face Dulzan had fallen in love with twenty years ago. It was the face she had once had, but had gradually grown out of without realizing it.

But now she had it back. Now Dulzan would be *hers* once more. She smiled.

She snatched the bread and wine from the girl and stuffed the bread into her mouth, still staring at the glass, its handle tight against the mug. Even with her mouth full of food, even chewing eagerly, she was beautiful.

"Satisfied?" The wizard's voice came from behind her, and she whirled to face him, wine sloshing over the rim of the mug and down the back of her hand.

"I think so," she admitted.

"Then remember, I want the rest of my fee in no more than two sixnights. Twenty-five rounds of gold."

"I remember," she said. "You'll get your money." She looked into the glass again. "I don't think Dulzan can resist *this*."

She was staring at her own image, but from the corner of her eye she thought she saw Poldrian grimace. She looked up, but his face was impassive and unreadable.

"Then I believe we are done, until you can pay me," he said.

"Yes," Sharra agreed. She swallowed the mouthful of bread, gulped the rest of the wine, then handed the apprentice the mirror and the empty mug. "I'll be back with your money," she said, as she headed for the street.

Outside the front door she paused, blinking in the bright morning sunlight, debating where to go first. It did not take long to decide; why delay? It was time to go to Dulzan's shop and get her husband back.

She made her way to South Street, and followed that from East-side to Crafton, where she turned onto Carpenter Street. A cool breeze was blowing up from the sea, and she wished she had a jacket, but then she caught herself. She did not want to conceal her restored charms. As long as she was not actually shivering or displaying gooseflesh, the more bare skin, the better – not that her clothing was indecent, by any means! She wore a very respectable blue satin tunic, with a gold-embroidered square neckline cut just slightly too low to be called modest, and three-quarter sleeves with oversize cuffs that she thought were charming. She had not worn a hat, since she had not been certain what the magic would involve, and that sea-breeze ruffled her hair gently without really mussing it.

She remembered what she had seen in the mirror. Dulzan would not be able to resist her, she was sure!

And then she was at the door of his shop. She did not hesitate, but flung it open and walked right in, her hips swinging just a little more than necessary.

Dulzan was bent down behind a chest of drawers, fitting something in place; he heard the tinkle of the bell and called, "I'll be right with you!" without looking up.

"Hello, Dulzan!" she called, in her most dulcet tones.

She thought he started slightly at the sound of her voice, but he finished whatever he was doing and wiped his hands on his apron before rising to look at her.

When he saw her he stared, clearly astonished. She stopped in the middle of the shop and posed for him, her hand on her hip, trying not to be too obvious about it. She smiled at him, and looked for any hint of desire in his eyes, but saw only surprise.

After several seconds of silence, Dulzan exclaimed, "Sharra, what did you *do*?"

"Whatever do you mean?" she asked with a smile, shifting her weight to her other foot.

"Is it a glamour? An illusion?"

"It's no illusion, Dulzan," she said, her voice sultry.

"Well, you didn't do *that* with your paints and powders! It's magic, isn't it?"

Sharra hesitated only the briefest of moments before deciding she could not hide the truth forever, and it would be best to admit it at once. "Yes, it's magic," she said. "I spent the money you gave me on a youth spell. I could see that you were tired of me, and when I looked in the mirror I could understand why, so I hired a wizard to restore me to that same young woman you fell in love with twenty years ago."

He stared at her silently for a moment more, then said, "But *I'm* not the young fool I was twenty years ago."

"No, you're a fine mature man," Sharra answered, taking a step toward him. "That's why I did this! So you could have the beauty you want and deserve."

Dulzan stepped back against the wall behind the chest of drawers, and shook his head. "Sharra, I want a fine mature *woman*. Which you have never been, and apparently, from what I see now, will never *be*." He frowned. "If you thought changing your appearance would be enough to make me change my mind, then you really haven't learned a thing in all the time we were married. It wasn't your *appearance* that mattered." His brows lowered. "I gave you that money to *live* on, Sharra, and now you've thrown it away on this stupid scheme that you should have *known* wouldn't work. I suggest you go get your money back and return to your old self, then go find someone else to marry you, because I am *not* taking you back, at *any* age!"

For a moment Sharra stood stunned, unable to believe what she was hearing. Then she dismissed it as absurd; what man could resist her? She sashayed forward, head lowered, eyes peering out from beneath lush lashes.

Dulzan straightened up, anger plain on his face.

"Are you *sure* you don't want me?" she murmured, rounding one side of the bureau and reaching out to put a hand on his chest.

He pushed it away. "Yes, I'm sure," he said.

"I promise that if you take me back, I won't disappoint you," she said. "I still remember everything I've learned; it's only my body that's young again."

"But that's the thing, Sharra," Dulzan said. "You never learned *anything*. I'm willing to wager that whatever you look like, you're still the same selfish nag you always were. I'm just sorry it took me so long to give up on you; I could have been enjoying my nights at home alone *years* ago, instead of listening to you whining and complaining and trying to turn me into your social mannequin, your tool to build your own status."

Her eyes widened. "But Dulzan...!"

"I didn't leave you because of your *looks*, Sharra. I left because of your tongue – your nagging, and your greed, and...and *everything about you*. All you cared about was yourself."

"I cared about *you*!"

"No, you didn't. You never even knew who I was. You wanted me to be the husband *you* wanted, and never considered what *I* wanted."

"What you wanted was stupid!" The instant the words were spoken Sharra regretted them, and clapped a dainty hand over her mouth.

Dulzan smiled for the first time since she entered the shop. "So you *did* know I didn't want to be your high-society puppet."

"No, I mean... Dulzan, please..." Her voice trailed off in confusion.

"Get out of my shop, Sharra." He pointed at the door. "Get out and don't come back. The way you look now you shouldn't have any trouble finding a new husband."

"But I want *you*..."

"Sharra, I am the one man in Ethshar of the Sands you can *never* have. Because I'm the one who knows you better than anyone else. Now go away, before I call a guardsman."

Sharra started to reach for him again, but he slapped her hand away. "Get out," he said.

"But Dulzan..."

"Out!" He grabbed her arm and spun her around, pointing her at the door.

"But you have to take me back!" she wailed. "I still owe the wizard money!"

Dulzan froze. "You what?"

"I didn't have enough to pay for it all at once!" she explained desperately, turning back to face him. "I need to pay the rest in the next twelvenight or he'll do something terrible to me! I thought you'd love me like this, and..."

"Sharra, *I* don't have any money! At least, not more than a few rounds. I gave you my life's savings. *All* of them. That wasn't enough? Blood and death, how much did this spell *cost*?"

She could not believe what she was hearing. To the best of her knowledge Dulzan, whatever his other failings, had never lied to her. Could he really have given her *all* his savings? That was mad!

"Your life's savings? But...why would you *do* that?"

"Because *you* care about money, and I don't! I knew I could earn more, but *you* never did an honest's day's work in your life, and I didn't want you to starve!"

Sharra started to protest that she had worked when she was an apprentice, but she did not want to let the conversation be diverted. She stammered for a moment, then said, "You don't have *any* more money hidden away?"

"No, I don't. Sharra, you need to go back to that wizard right away. How much do you owe him?"

"Twenty-five rounds of gold."

"Twenty-five..." His jaw dropped. When he could speak again, he said, "Sharra, what have you *done*?"

"I've sold our house and spent all your money to get you back, Dulzan. If I don't pay him he's going to do something horrible. You have to save me!"

For a moment Dulzan did not reply. His lips tightened. At last he said, "No. I don't. Not any more. You brought this on yourself, Sharra. I don't have any more gold; I already gave you all I had. I couldn't help you if I wanted to. I'd ask if you've gone mad, but honestly, I'm not sure you were ever sane. I'm not taking you back, and I don't have any money to give you. It sounds to me as if you have two sixnights to find yourself a rich fool, and I'd suggest you start looking *right now*." He turned her around again and gave her a push, and she stumbled toward the door. Trying to salvage what little dignity she still had, she lifted her head and walked out to the street without another word.

But once she had left the shop her shoulders sagged and she looked around desperately. What could she do now? She had nowhere to go; she had handed the buyer the keys to her house when she left for Poldrian's workshop. She had told him she would send for her belongings once she was settled in her new home, but she had assumed that would be Dulzan's place.

That clearly wasn't going to happen. At least, not in time to save her. She might be able to wear down his resistance in time, but not in a mere twelvenight.

At least she still had her family. She turned and headed for Weaver Street.

A moment later she walked into her parents' shop. Her father was behind the counter, writing in a ledger; her mother was nowhere in sight, but Sharra could hear the steady thumping of the big loom in the back room.

"Papa," she said, "I'm in trouble."

Her father looked up from the ledger, then started. "Sharra? Is that you?"

"Of course it is!"

"But you… What *happened* to you?"

"I bought a youth spell," she said. "And now I can't pay for it, and the wizard says he'll do something terrible if I don't find the money."

Kelder put down the pen. "What?"

"I need twenty-five rounds of *gold* by the eighth of Harvest!"

"*What*? Start at the beginning, Sharra."

She struggled to control herself when what she really wanted to do was fling herself at her father and sob into his chest. She stood up straight, took a deep breath, and said, "Dulzan left me."

"I know *that*, Sharra."

"Well, I wanted him back. I still love him – "

"No, you don't," her father interrupted.

"What?" Sharra asked, startled out of her planned explanation.

"You don't love him. I've known that for years, after watching you two together. You wanted him because he was big and strong and handsome and a master of his craft, someone you could show off, but you never loved him. I saw the way you two looked at one another, and I know what I *didn't* see – I didn't see love. If you want him back it's because he hurt your pride when he left."

"I *do* love him!" she protested, raising her head. "I always did!"

Kelder shook his head. "Maybe you really think so. I'm not going to argue. Go on."

Sharra hesitated. She *wanted* to argue, to insist that of course they loved each other and anyone who didn't think so just didn't understand, but she didn't want to let the conversation go wandering off course. She took a deep breath, and continued.

"Anyway," she said, "I thought he had lost interest because I wasn't young and beautiful anymore, so I decided to *do* something about it. I took all the money he'd given me, and all the money I could raise elsewhere, and I sold our house, and that came to a little less than sixty rounds of gold, and I took that to a wizard named Poldrian of Morningside and bought a youth spell. He just finished it this morning. But I promised I'd pay him another twenty-five rounds once Dulzan took me back; I was *sure* that if Dulzan gave me almost thirty rounds of gold that he must have more hidden away for himself."

"Why would you think…" Her father stopped and shook his head. "Never mind. Go on."

"When I left the wizard's shop today I went straight to Dulzan, and he threw me out! He says he doesn't want me no matter what I look like, and he doesn't have any more gold, and he couldn't help me even if he wanted to, and I think it's true."

Sharra watched as conflicting emotions distorted her father's features, ending finally in a look of resignation.

"Sharra," he said, "you've always thought you're smarter than everyone else, and sometimes you really *are* clever, but this time you have been *unbelievably* stupid! No, I take that back – it's completely believable, because it's just like you. Did you really think it was your *looks* that chased Dulzan away?"

"I…no, not… I mean, I didn't think I was *ugly* or anything, but I thought if I was really *beautiful* again, that would be enough to bring him back."

"Looks aren't everything, Sharra. You're thirty-eight; you ought to know that by now."

"I didn't…" Her shoulders sagged. "I was *wrong*, Papa; is that what you want me to say? I thought it would all be simple and easy. It's not. I can see now that if I want Dulzan back I need more than a youth spell, but right now, this is what I *have*, and I need to pay for it or the wizard is going to do something horrible to me."

"And the magistrates will allow it, because it's a legitimate debt," her father agreed.

Sharra nodded. "I signed a contract." She bit her lip, afraid she might start crying. "So what can I do? Do you and Mama have any gold you can lend me? Or maybe Dallisa or Nerra?"

Kelder snorted. "Sharra, your mother is a weaver, not a wizard! And I'm just a merchant, buying her supplies and selling her products. *We* don't have any gold; our entire savings are in silver, and not enough to even *begin* to pay your bill. Unless they've been hiding secrets, your sisters don't have it, either. *You* were always the successful one, you and Dulzan, with your parties at the overlord's palace and your house in Brightside and your gold-embroidered tunics. Dalissa was so jealous of you!"

Sharra knew that was true; she had reveled in it, gloating quietly whenever she saw her sisters – or sometimes not so quietly. It was one reason she hadn't seen her sisters very often; they had resented her behavior.

She had always thought they avoided her because they didn't like to be reminded of their own relative failure, but somewhere in the back of her mind a little voice suggested that maybe those two weren't really failures at all, they had just found her air of superiority obnoxious.

That was another distraction, though. She needed to stay focused.

"Is there anywhere we could *borrow* the money?"

"Twenty-five rounds of gold, by the eighth of Harvest?" He shook his head. "I don't think so. Even if we put the shop up as surety – twenty-five rounds of gold? I don't think so."

"I still have almost eight rounds left; I thought I might need it for clothes, or to pay for a wedding. So I only really need seventeen more."

"That might as well be a thousand."

"But then what can I *do*?" Sharra wailed, her fragile composure vanishing completely.

"You can go back and talk to the wizard," he replied. "Tell him you made a mistake and you want your money back."

"He won't do that. He warned me, but I didn't listen."

"Well, then ask for more time to come up with the money! I don't think you can get Dulzan back, and I'm sure he really doesn't have the money anyway, but you're a lovely girl – again – and maybe you can find someone who will help."

"*Talk* to him?"

"Why not? Really, could it make anything worse?"

Sharra considered that, and honestly did not see any way talking to Poldrian could hurt her situation. And the spell had not really worked, after all – she had wanted Dulzan back, and she hadn't gotten him.

He had *cheated* her, in a way, not warning her that it might not work!

Except he had asked her repeatedly if she was really sure. He had told her it wasn't a love spell.

But he should have just *told* her it wouldn't work, and he hadn't! He should have pressed harder, but he had wanted a victim to test his spells on. Surely she could talk him into letting her off, or giving her more time, or *something*.

"Thank you, Papa," she said. She leaned over and kissed his cheek – something she had not done in many years, but her youthful body made it easy to return to youthful habits. Then she straightened up, managed an approximation of a smile, turned, and left, marching out into the sunlit street.

She had not noticed that the clacking of the loom in the back room had stopped during the conversation with her father. Once she was out of the shop, with the door closed behind her, her mother emerged from the back of the shop.

"What was all that?" she asked her husband. "I heard part of it. I didn't want to barge in, where she sounded so upset."

Kelder sighed. "Our little troublemaker has really done it this time," he said. "Sit down, and I'll tell you everything she said."

CHAPTER SIX

Sharra leaned around the door of Poldrian's shop. "Hello?" she called. She did not see anyone in the front room. The apprentice who usually greeted her was not there. She stepped in. "*Hello*?"

There was a muffled "thud" from beyond the door to the back. Frowning, Sharra crossed the room and rapped her knuckles on the wooden door. "Hello?" she called again.

She heard voices, and then the door opened and Poldrian appeared, his hair and beard in disarray and wearing no hat.

"Oh, it's you," he said. "You're back already? Do you have the rest of my fee?"

"No," Sharra said, head up and voice firm. "It didn't work. I want my money back."

Poldrian frowned. "That isn't happening. I warned you. The spell worked, and you're young and beautiful again, and you owe me another twenty-five rounds of gold. You signed the contract."

"But Dulzan won't take me back!"

"That is not my problem. I never thought he would, but *you* insisted he would. I gave you several chances to change your mind, and you went through with it, so I suggest you find some other way of getting my money."

"But I didn't get what I wanted! Why should I pay you?"

"Because I cast a rare and very difficult spell for you, and I never promised it would help you get your man back. I'm sorry it didn't, but you still owe me the rest of the price."

"I can't pay it!" Sharra wailed, her bravado collapsing. "I can get maybe another eight rounds, but I won't have anything left to live on, and I can't find seventeen more!"

"Well, you better start looking again, because if you don't pay me by the eighth of Harvest, I'll test out a spell on you. As I told you, there's a petrifaction spell I've wanted to try."

"You'll turn me to stone? Over *money*?"

"I'll turn you to stone, yes. You'll make a very attractive statue, my dear."

"You wouldn't dare!"

Poldrian sighed. "Of course I would," he said

"If I'm turned to stone, you'll never get your money!"

"It seems very unlikely that I'll get it if you *aren't* turned to stone, either."

Sharra took a deep breath, realized she had no idea what to say, and spluttered wordlessly. Then she stopped.

"Fine," she said. "Then take your stupid youth spell back!"

Poldrian laughed outright at that. "You idiot," he said. "I couldn't even if I wanted to; the magic doesn't work like that. I told you there's no counter-spell. This isn't an illusion or a glamour or an enchantment; you really *are* twenty years younger, and turning you back to your old self wouldn't mean breaking a spell, it would mean casting another spell, an aging spell, and I don't *know* any aging spells. I'm not sure there *are* any; I mean, why would anyone want to be older?"

"But can't you…there must be some way…"

He cocked his head to one side and stroked his beard thoughtfully. "There *are* a few reversal spells that *might* work, but they're pretty difficult and expensive all by themselves, on top of what you already owe me."

"I shouldn't owe you anything! I paid you fifty rounds of gold!"

"And that wasn't enough. You wanted a youth spell. I cast a youth spell. We agreed on a price, and you said you'd pay it. Now, pay it, or wind up as an ornament somewhere. You're a beautiful young woman; maybe you still have time to seduce some rich old fool. Even if you can't get your husband back, you ought to be able to get *someone*."

"I'm not a whore!"

"That's good, because no one would pay that much for a whore. Listen, if it's any comfort, the petrifaction spell will be reversible if I do it right, and if anyone ever pays me what you owe me, I'll try to turn you back. In fact, I won't even charge anything more for it, because I want to see whether it works. Do you have any family who might pay off the bill eventually?"

"Maybe," Sharra said. Then reality caught up with her, for once. Her face fell. "No," she admitted. "Twenty-five rounds of gold? None of them could ever pay that much."

"Then I suggest you start looking for another source of funds. Now, if you don't mind, I have other business to attend to." He started to turn away.

Desperate, Sharra tried to grab for the knife on his belt, but found that her fingers could not grip it; they slid away as if the leather hilt was some impossible liquid. Then she felt a grip like iron close on her wrist.

"Now, *that* was silly," Poldrian said, as he lifted her arm away from the weapon. "Hasn't anyone ever told you not to touch a wizard's dagger?" He released her, and she stared at the red marks his fingers had left. "I understand that you're under a great deal of stress, facing an eternity as a lump of stone, but I really think you had better leave right now, and not come back without the rest of my fee."

She stared at him for a moment, and then turned and fled.

A hundred feet down the street from his door she stopped and took a deep breath to calm herself. She stood there, eyes closed, trying to think of a way out of her predicament.

Dulzan wasn't going to help her. It appeared her parents weren't going to help her, either. Who did that leave?

There were her sisters, but she didn't think either of them had much money, or that they would loan it to her if they did. Dalissa probably had *some* money, but was unlikely to let any of it go, and it surely wouldn't be enough to really matter.

Friends – she realized with horror that she hardly *had* any friends. She had had neighbors in Brightside she spoke with regularly and sometimes accompanied to parties and concerts, but she had never been very close with any of them.

She had spent some time with Dulzan's friends and customers – as little as possible, but some – but she knew that they were *Dulzan's* friends and customers. They would side with him, not with her.

Or maybe they would help her to prevent Dulzan from being embarrassed. After all, she and Dulzan were technically still married, as it had not yet been anywhere near a year and a day since Dulzan left.

She had had her own friends once, back when she and Dulzan lived in Crafton – not very many, but a few, people like Desset. When she tried to think of one she could call on for help, though, she realized that she had hardly seen any of them in years, and could not even be sure where most of them lived anymore.

There were her social contacts at the palace and among the city's elite, but she was not so foolish as to think any of them were true friends who would loan her rounds of gold. The women she had met and talked to at fancy parties weren't so much friends as rivals, constantly trying to impress and outdo one another, and she could not think of any of them who might be generous enough to help her. Much of her standing with them had been based on the belief that *she* was rich, when in fact it had taken most of Dulzan's earnings – well, most of the earnings she had known about, anyway – just to maintain appearances.

How *had* he managed to save up all that gold, anyway? And here she had thought he wasted what little money he kept from her on beer.

She might be able to borrow money here and there, from her sisters and friends, but she did not for a moment imagine that it would amount to even half the seventeen rounds of gold she needed.

Was there some magic she could use to raise the money?

She opened her eyes and looked along Wizard Street. The only magicians she had spoken to in years, beyond small talk at palace parties, were Poldrian and Mother Maffi. Maffi had been helpful with certain matters, but Sharra knew that was because Sharra had paid her, not because they were friends. If Maffi had a way to acquire large sums of gold on short notice, she would hardly have been selling health aids and contraceptive spells from a dingy little shop. Even though that shop was only a few blocks away, Sharra did not turn in that direction.

But, Sharra realized, she *did* have some magic to work with. She was, to all appearances, young and beautiful, but with the mind and experience of a middle-aged woman. Poldrian had suggested she seduce a rich man – maybe she actually could. That wasn't what she had *wanted* to do with her restored youth, but it might work.

She had met plenty of wealthy men at the palace; was there one who might be susceptible to her charms? She frowned, thinking hard.

Most of them were already married, of course, and she was not aware that any of them were looking for a second wife. Some might consider a little fling; she knew that Orzik the Vintner had been seen in the company of whores, and Lord Varl, with his broad shoulders and winning smile, was said to have bedded several of the palace servants.

But as she had told Poldrian, she wasn't a whore, nor was she a serving girl, and she doubted that any of those women had ever gotten any gold from Orzik or Lord Varl, nor enough silver to equal a golden bit.

What about single men, though? There *were* a few, after all, and many of them were definitely interested in women – or at least they certainly claimed to be. She started a mental list of names, and bit her lip – they were all so young!

But then, she realized, so was she, now. And a man's youth and inexperience might make him more suggestible, more easily misled, for a woman of thirty-eight who looked to be eighteen.

But she could not very well go to any man she knew and admit she was the wife of Dulzan the Cabinetmaker, and then try to seduce him – not even when Dulzan had left her. She would need to assume a new identity.

That should not be difficult, though. She could claim to be her own niece, Sharra the Younger, just now trying to enter high society. That could work, she thought. But she would have to act quickly, to win a man over by the eighth of Harvest.

She would need the right sort of clothing. Most of her clothes were still in the house she had sold, but most of them weren't really the sort of thing an eighteen-year-old woman would be wearing on her first visit to the overlord's palace. Most particularly, they weren't the sort of thing that would draw the attention, but not the suspicion, of a wealthy young man like Halzin of Nightside, or Sindel Galeth's son.

And she would need more than one outfit. If she was going to play the role of a wealthy young woman who could be trusted with large sums of money, and not just a beggar, she would need to look the part for several days.

But her mother was a weaver specializing in expensive fabrics, and her sister Dalissa was an excellent seamstress. Even if Dalissa alone couldn't manage to do enough in the limited time available, finding someone else who could sew would not be *that* difficult.

She turned and headed back toward Weaver Street.

CHAPTER SEVEN

Sharra smiled as the dance ended, and curtsied to her partner, but she knew the smile was a little strained. She hoped Sindel wouldn't notice.

He seemed a nice enough boy, really, though she would have thought a man of twenty would be more mature, and more sure of himself. Apparently Galeth the Merchant had coddled his son. Given enough time, Sharra was fairly sure she could talk her way into his bed and his strongbox.

But she didn't *have* enough time. It was the sixth of Harvest, and she needed that sixteen rounds in no more than two days, and the stress was telling on her.

Really, she knew she should be grateful that her friends and family – well, mostly Dulzan's friends and her family, actually – had managed to raise even a portion of a single round of gold. She had wheedled, begged, and pleaded every day, going from friend to friend, and after she had finished that depressingly short list she had gone from acquaintance to acquaintance; she had put all her belongings up for sale, as well. She now had nine rounds and one bit in gold, and five rounds in silver, tucked away under the mattress in the back room of her parents' shop.

Dulzan's sister Banni had been the most generous, donating a full round of silver; that had surprised Sharra, since she knew Banni had never liked her. They had not even spoken since Sharra bought the house in Brightside, but a round of silver, nevertheless.

Not that it was anywhere near enough. Sharra knew she needed to raise far more.

And every evening she had gone to whatever social events she could, trying to lure a man into giving her the rest. Her mother had provided the finest fabrics, her sister Dallisa had grudgingly sewn her gowns, and she had certainly drawn plenty of male interest – and even some female interest, a possibility she had not anticipated. She had attended banquets and wine-tasting parties and now this dance, held by the whimsical Lord Vashar and his Tintallionese dancing master.

She had not, however, managed to entrap a single wealthy lover. She had discovered that after twenty years of marriage, she did not remember how romance really worked. Her skill at serious flirting, rather than the sort of empty playfulness expected of pretty women, was hopelessly rusty. Much of her small talk was meant for a different audience, and she had trouble feigning interest in the callow youths who should have been her natural prey.

For a few days she thought she might have been able to capture the affections of Balash of Grandgate, a widower in his forties, which she thought that would have been a *perfect* pairing, but she had apparently said something wrong, and now he was avoiding her. Sindel, young as he was, appeared to be her best remaining option. He seemed willing to believe that her similarity to the older woman he had met a month or two back was merely a family resemblance, but while he was plainly very interested in her body, he seemed to draw away at even the most casual mention of money.

She wondered whether she might let him take her to bed, and then try to rob the house while he slept. He and his parents probably did not leave the family fortune just lying around, though; their gold was most likely in a hidden strongbox somewhere, bolted to a wall or floor. Or it might even be held in trust by some loyal friend, safely out of sight but ready to be retrieved on demand. Ethshar of the Sands did have its share of professional burglars, after all.

This was all foreign to her, though. She had always acquired money by having someone *give* it to her, not by stealing it. She had thought she would be able to do that, and indeed she had been given a necklace and two silver bracelets by some of her new admirers, but those had not amounted to even half a round of gold when sold. She did not have *time* to raise the money in dribs and drabs of that sort.

"I have greatly enjoyed your company, Sharra," Sindel said, as he straightened from his own bow. "I could almost think I felt some of the magic the ritual dancers use, in that last piece."

"And I have enjoyed your company, as well," she replied, trying unsuccessfully to blush. She had not felt any magic beyond the pleasure of her own youthful vigor, but did not want to discourage the man.

"Perhaps the magic was entirely in the company, rather than the dance," Sindel said. "Would you care to accompany me for a walk, so that we might see if it lingers?"

"I would be delighted," she said, trying to broaden her smile.

He led her to the door of the hall, where they both said a quick farewell to Lord Vashar and stepped out in the street.

"Which way shall we go?" Sindel asked.

"Perhaps toward your home?" Sharra suggested.

"Oh, no, I don't think so," Sindel replied. "It's too early for that."

She was unsure how he meant that, and decided not to risk saying the wrong thing. "Then I leave it to you, sir," she said. "Where would *you* like to go?"

"Perhaps *your* home?"

Sharra hesitated as she tried to think of the best response. Then she said, "My home is in Ethshar of the Rocks, and I think that's too far for a casual walk."

"Ah, of course. But where are you staying in *this* Ethshar?"

"With my par…with my grandparents, on Weaver Street. Which I think is hardly a suitable place for a stroll at this hour."

"Nonsense! I don't believe I have ever seen Weaver Street; show me the way!"

Again, Sharra did not immediately know what to say. She did not want a rich man's son to see her sad little mattress in her parents' shop, but she did not want to anger him by being uncooperative, either. She *needed* to keep his interest. "If that's really what you want," she said, gesturing to the right.

She took a circuitous route, hoping that she could suggest a better destination, but the more she tried to suggest other places they might go, the more Sindel insisted on seeing her "grandparents'" home. At last she could delay no longer, and they arrived at the door beneath the sign reading KIRSHA THE WEAVER, FINE FABRICS. The shop window was dark.

"This is your grandparents' home?" Sindel asked, looking up and down the street. It was largely deserted; customers generally wanted sunlight to see the colors of the cloth they were buying, and there were no taverns or other businesses on Weaver Street that would attract the residents after hours. Street lamps cast an orange glow across the storefronts, and several upstairs windows were lit, but the two of them were the only strollers in sight.

Sharrra said, "Yes."

"And this Kirsha?"

"My grandmother," she replied.

"Your grandmother is a weaver?" His arm, which had been around her waist, fell away.

"Yes, she is." She bit off a defensive, "Is anything wrong with that?" She knew perfectly well that Sindel would not think weaving was a worthy occupation; for the past twenty years, *she* had not thought it was.

"And your grandfather?"

"A traveling merchant." *That*, at least, was a calling Sindel would respect, since his father was one, albeit a hundred times more successful than her own father.

Sindel seemed about to say something more, but apparently thought better of it. "I must meet them, then," he said, and before Sharra could react, he had knocked loudly on the door of the shop.

Sharra grabbed for his arm. "They might be asleep!" she said, though the hour was not really all that late.

"They aren't waiting up for their granddaughter?"

"No! I'm a grown woman, and they trust me to look out for myself!"

He smiled at her. "And do you have magics, then, to protect you from an attacker?"

That seemed an oddly cruel and cynical question, but Sharra was spared the necessity of an answer when the shop door opened and a young man, roughly Sindel's own age, looked out.

"Aunt Sharra?" he said. "Is that you?"

Sharra turned to look at him, startled. It took her a few seconds to recognize the youth.

During those few seconds, Sindel said, "*Aunt* Sharra?" He turned to her and asked, astonished, "You have a grown nephew?"

"My sister is much older than I am," Sharra said, hoping Dallisa would forgive the lie. She had at last figured out who this was. "Lador? What are *you* doing here?"

"I came to see if I could help," he said. "I heard you needed money." He looked at Sindel. "Who is this?"

"Sindel Galeth's son," Sindel replied, with a deep bow. "And you are...?"

"Lador the Weaver," Lador replied. "Aunt Sharra?"

"I...am glad to see you," Sharra managed. "Sindel and I were out for a walk."

"And now I have seen you safely home," Sindel said, stepping away from her. "I will say good night, and be on my way. Alas, that I cannot help you with the money this fellow says you need!"

"Oh, but Lador has been misinformed..." she began, but then she stopped. It was too late now; she could not possibly expect Sindel to give her anything. He had undoubtedly already realized the truth, that Sharra's interest had been entirely in his money, and not himself. She might still pursue him, and perhaps wind up with an agreeable bedmate, but there was no way he would provide the sixteen gold rounds that would prevent her petrifaction.

"Has he?" Sindel asked, taking another step away. "Tell me, is your appearance a glamour?"

"No," Sharra said. "This is really me. I swear it by all the gods."

"And will you swear that you aren't interested in my father's money?"

She sighed, realizing it was hopeless. "No, I can't swear to that. But I meant you no ill, I promise; *that* I can honestly say. Good night, Sindel; I hope you can find yourself a more suitable woman." She stepped up to the door and took her nephew by the arm. "Come on, Lador. Let the man go about his business."

"Good night, Sharra," Sindel said.

And then she and Lador were inside the shop, and she closed the door behind them.

The heavy curtains were drawn, so no light had shown on the street, but three oil lamps were burning on the shelf behind the counter, and a ledger was open on the counter itself. Sharra took this in, then turned to Lador and asked, "What's going on here?"

"Oh, well, I was going over the books," Lador said. "I've been talking to Grandmother and Grandfather about joining the business here, and I wanted to see how things stand." He hesitated, then added, "I was also hoping to find some overlooked accounts that we might collect, to help you pay the wizard."

"So you really did come here to help me?"

"Well, partly. But I've been traveling for the past three years, working in one shop or another, or taking odd jobs, and I was tired of it. Being a *literal* journeyman is not for me. I wanted to come home and work in my home town again, and when I got Mama's message that you were in trouble, I decided this was the time." He glanced at the closed door. "I said something wrong, didn't I?" he asked. "You were hoping to get some money from that man."

"Yes, I was," Sharra admitted. "About the only thing I have left to make money is my looks, so I've been looking for a rich...a rich husband."

"I'm so sorry, Aunt Sharra! I didn't know." After a brief pause he added, "You *do* look beautiful, though."

"Given how much I paid for that stupid spell, I would hope so!"

"But it was a youth spell, wasn't it? Not a beauty spell."

"That's right. I was beautiful when I was young."

"And now you are again! But you still need to pay for the spell, don't you?"

"I need to *finish* paying for it. I *did* pay for most of it, but I didn't have enough for the entire price."

"Mama told me that. You still need twenty-five rounds of gold."

Sharra did not feel like explaining that she had accumulated about a third of it. For one thing, if she did, and got petrified anyway, Dallisa would probably try to steal it. Or Nerra would, or Lador, or someone, or they would fight over it, or divide it up, and she did not want any of them to get it. "Something like that," she said.

"That's a lot of money."

"Yes, it is."

"Does that Sindel person really have that much?"

"I'm pretty sure his father does. And I hadn't gotten anywhere with anyone else."

"I've been trying to think of some way to help, but I haven't come up with anything. How soon do you need it?"

"By tomorrow night," Sharra replied.

"Oh," Lador said, staring. "Oh, that's bad."

"I know," Sharra said.

"You don't think the wizard will give you more time?"

"No, I don't," she snapped.

"Oh." He glanced at the open ledger. "I was almost done with the accounts; should I finish up, or just go back to Mama's place and leave you alone?"

"Go ahead and finish up, though I doubt you'll find enough unpaid bills to be any use."

"I haven't found *any* yet."

Sharra was disappointed by that, but not surprised. Her parents had never been careless about such things. "Are your grandparents around?"

"Grandmother is upstairs; I'm not sure about Grandfather."

"Thank you. Go on back to Dallisa, then, and tell her I appreciate her writing to you."

He hesitated, then headed for the door. "I'll see you tomorrow, Aunt Sharra," he said.

She watched him leave, then headed for the back room and the stairs.

CHAPTER EIGHT

Sharra spent most of the seventh of Harvest waiting for a miracle – for an unknown debtor to show up with a basket of gold for her parents, for Dulzan to find another hidden cache he had forgotten, for Sindel to come to the shop apologizing for his rudeness and asking how much she needed, *anything* that might give her the money she needed.

No miracle happened.

Lador had finally figured out just how much harm he had done with his careless words, and spent half the day apologizing, which did not help Sharra's mood at all. Her sister Nerra had had the idea of finding something really valuable to sell to a wizard – if not Poldrian, then another – and had gone searching through junk shops and waste-heaps in hopes of finding a misplaced vial of dragon's blood or some other priceless ingredient for a wizard's spells. Dallisa had asked a friend who belonged to a troupe of ritual dancers whether they could help, and while they had no specific dance to pay off debts, they could and did attempt a generalized blessing that would bring Sharra good fortune – eventually, and if no stronger magic prevented it.

The dancers readily admitted a petrifaction spell was stronger magic, but the dance couldn't *hurt*, and they would not charge her, only ask that if she did survive and thrive, she might donate to them in the future.

Sharra sometimes wondered why ritual dancers bothered with their art, since the magical effects were generally so weak and un-reliable, and they didn't charge a set fee but merely passed around a leather bag for donations; she had concluded they must just like dancing.

More than one well-meaning idiot suggested she stop her use-less struggling and simply enjoy her last day of life; so far she had resisted the urge to punch such people in the nose, but it got more difficult each time.

Finally, when the sun had set and no fabulous stroke of fortune had come to save her from her doom, she put on the best and most revealing of her new dresses and made her way to Wizard Street, with a still-apologetic Lador accompanying her for moral support, to plead for mercy.

Poldrian refused to see her. The apprentice – whose name, Sharra realized, she had never learned – let her in the front door, but told her that the wizard would not allow her any further into his home, and that he had no intention of speaking with her.

"I'm sorry," the apprentice said, "but he *did* warn you, and you insisted."

"I have *most* of the money!" Sharra lied. Then she caught herself. "Well, part of it, anyway, maybe not *most*. But I can get the rest if he gives me more time!"

The apprentice turned up an empty palm. "I'm afraid it's all or nothing. If your friends and family come up with the rest, he'll turn you back – or at least he says he'll *try*. I'm pretty sure he's never reversed a petrifaction spell before."

Sharra turned to Lador. "You heard that? Keep raising money!"

"Of course, Aunt Sharra."

Then she turned back to the apprentice. "I'm not leaving until he sees me! I need a chance to talk to him!"

"And *I* need to obey my master's orders," the apprentice replied. "He said to remind you that there are worse things than being turned to stone with a reversible spell, and that breaking into a wizard's home would justify using them. Honestly, Sharra, he isn't just making idle threats; he has some spells in his book that *terrify* me. And if I disobey him, he could use them on *me*."

Sharra stared at her for a moment, then burst into tears. It was all too much. Dulzan had left her and Poldrian had cheated her and Sindel had deserted her and her family had failed her and now she was going to be turned to stone and she didn't understand *why* nobody liked her, why they were mistreating her so. She was beautiful and vivacious and had only wanted the best for Dulzan, but even the friends who had given or loaned her money said they were only doing it for Dulzan, even her own family said they were helping because she was family, no one had even *pretended* they were helping out of love for her – well, no one but her parents. Even Lador, who had come to confront the wizard with her, was here out of guilt for ruining her chances with Sindel, and had come back to Weaver Street not for love of her, but to join her mother's business.

What had she ever done that was so wrong?

"Your master is a *monster*!" she shouted. "A monster! How can he just *murder* me in cold blood?"

"It's not murder, you know that, and you owe him a *ridiculous* amount of money you've refused to pay."

"I don't *have* it!"

"Then you shouldn't have promised to pay it! You shouldn't have signed the contract!"

The apprentice was visibly upset, and clearly starting to lose her temper. Sharra stopped yelling and flopped onto one of the settees, still weeping.

Lador sat on a nearby chair, looking around worriedly, clearly unsure what he should be doing. The apprentice, after a few moments, went back to reading the book she kept behind the podium, though she glanced up every so often to see whether Sharra was still there and still weeping.

No matter how miserable one is, Sharra discovered, it's difficult to keep crying indefinitely. After perhaps half an hour, perhaps less, the tears stopped; after another ten minutes or so the sniffling and sobbing ceased, as well. She sat a little longer, staring down at her hands, then looked up.

"Do you have a handkerchief?" she asked.

To her surprise, it was Lador who handed her a square of fine linen. "It's one of my samples," he explained apologetically. "I'm still a journeyman, after all."

"It's fine," she said. "Thank you." She wiped her eyes and cheeks, then blew her nose and handed the cloth back.

She set her mouth firmly, then said, "Apprentice? Tell Poldrian I'm not leaving until he speaks to me, no matter how long it takes."

"I'll tell him," the apprentice said. She closed her book and set it aside. "Wait here," she said. Then she slipped through the door at the back.

Sharra had lost track of time, and had dozed off from nervous exhaustion, when Lador remarked, "She's been gone a long time, hasn't she?"

Sharra started awake and looked up. The apprentice still had not returned; she and Lador were alone in the wizard's front room. She leaned over to peer out the narrow front window.

The streetlights were lit – some with normal oil, but some, since this was Wizard Street, with magic glowing in various colors. There were no pedestrians in sight, and the shop across the street had a "Closed" sign on the door.

"What time is it?" Sharra asked.

"I don't know," Lador said, "but it's very late."

Sharra frowned, then quickly erased the frown – she knew it wasn't the cute sort of frown that men found attractive, and if Poldrian were to appear suddenly she wanted to look as endearing, as charming, as possible, so that he might take pity on her. She got to her feet.

And then Poldrian was there, stepping out of thin air. She whirled to face him, while Lador gaped like a fish.

"My apprentice tells me you won't leave until I speak to you," the wizard said. "So I am speaking to you, because the gods know I don't want you in my parlor forever!"

"Lord Wizard!" Sharra exclaimed, though she knew that was not an appropriate form of address – by Guild law, lords could not be wizards and wizards could not be lords. "Please, take pity on me! Give me more time!"

"Do you have my money?"

"Not all of it, but I have almost half!"

Lador started. "You do?"

"Nine rounds!" Sharra exclaimed.

"That's the best you could do?"

"I need more time! I'm sure I can find a man who will…" She let the sentence trail off.

"You think so?"

"I do!"

"You've had almost a twelvenight."

"That's not…it takes time!"

"Show me why you think you can talk a man into giving you so much gold."

For a moment Sharra did not understand, and then a wild hope burst into her heart. He wanted to see her be alluring! If she could seduce *him*, then all her worries would be over. He had not seemed interested before, but perhaps he had been thinking of her, remembering her beauty, these past two sixnights!

She put a hand on her hip and bent one knee forward, cocked her head a little to one side and put on a smile...

And the room began to fade away. She could not move to adjust her position – or to do anything else. Her hand was frozen to her hip, her lips locked into a smile, her head permanently tilted, as her vision went dark and the world turned black. She did not understand what was happening; why couldn't she move? Why couldn't she see anything? She couldn't *feel* anything, either.

But she could still hear. "Oh, gods! Blood and death!" she heard Lador exclaim. "You did it!!"

"Did you doubt I would?" Poldrian's voice said.

"I thought she had another day!"

"It's more than an hour past midnight, young man; this is the eighth of Harvest, and I said she had *until* the eighth of Harvest, not to the end of the day."

"But she...she's my aunt, and I promised my mother I'd help her, and now she's a statue!"

"She's been turned to stone, yes."

For a few seconds no one spoke, and Sharra struggled to move, to see, but she could do nothing. She was frozen in utter darkness.

"I never saw stone that color before," Lador said.

Sharra was no longer really fully conscious, but she wondered what had prompted Lador to remark on something so trivial in the face of such an atrocity.

"I think it's chalcedony," Poldrian said. "But I'm not sure. I'm not a sculptor or a jeweler, and the spell doesn't specify." There was a pause, and then he added, "I'll try to turn her back if someone pays the twenty-five rounds of gold she owes me. No additional charge for the reversal spell."

"I don't...we don't *have* twenty-five rounds of gold. I didn't even know she had *nine*. It must be hidden away somewhere."

"You think she was telling the truth?"

"I...I don't know. But why would she give a number like nine, if she was lying? Why not say twenty?"

"That's a good point. Maybe someday you can ask her."

"No, wait! You can't leave! What am I supposed to do now? I can't just *leave* her here like that!"

"Give my apprentice the address, and we'll have her delivered to her home. Now, good night. It's been a long day, and I'm tired. My apprentice will see you out." Sharra thought she might have heard a door close.

"This way," the apprentice's voice said.

"But…the address. She… Kirsha the Weaver, on Weaver Street."

"Kirsha the Weaver," the apprentice repeated. "When should we have her delivered?"

"*I* don't know," Lador said. "Tomorrow, maybe?"

"We'll see," the apprentice said.

Then Sharra heard footsteps, and a door closing, and then silence.

Even in her half-asleep state, Sharra was puzzled that she had heard *anything* after the spell took effect. If she had been turned to stone, why wasn't she dead? How could she live without breathing? Without a heartbeat? But she was still here.

Could she still hear? Everything was quiet now; was that because the others had all left, or because the transformation was more nearly complete? Maybe she wasn't entirely stone yet, and would gradually fade away as the rest of her changed.

She wondered why she wasn't panicking, why she wasn't thoroughly terrified by her situation. Perhaps her emotions had been petrified along with her body, even while her mind lingered.

She stood motionless, not knowing what to expect, not knowing whether she would survive, but comforted by Poldrian's promise to restore her to life once her family had paid his fee. She knew it might take years, but surely, they would raise the money eventually! Dulzan was still a highly-sought-after master cabinetmaker; her mother was a well-regarded master weaver, and her father a competent, if not wildly successful, merchant. Even Lador, though he was a mere journeyman now, would probably be able to earn some extra money eventually. Her sisters, her nieces – they had all said they wanted to help. Sooner or later, she would be turned back.

She hoped it wouldn't take too long.

Sharra had dozed off, unsure whether she would ever wake again, but she was startled awake by a loud thump.

"There you go," an unfamiliar voice said.

"He really did it," her father's voice said.

"Did you think he wouldn't?" said the voice of Poldrian's apprentice.

"I don't... I *hoped* he wouldn't. I know she owed him a lot of money she couldn't pay, but I hoped he would take pity on her, or at least give her more time."

"He wanted to make a point," the apprentice said. "Besides, she annoyed him. She was rude and abrasive, and she originally said she wanted a love spell and then changed it to a youth spell instead, and then when he tried to get rid of her by naming an outrageous price, she *agreed* to it without even trying to bargain him down!"

"She did?" Lador's voice asked.

"She never even asked what any of the other spells would cost; she just picked the most expensive, and didn't balk when he told her a price half again what it should have been."

"Wait," her father said. "You mean it should have only been *fifty* rounds of gold, instead of seventy-five?"

"Well, maybe sixty. The ingredients aren't cheap, and it really is a very difficult spell. Dangerous, too, though more for the subject than the wizard casting it. But seventy-five was just an opening offer, and then she accepted it, and signed a contract agreeing to it."

Sharra would have blinked, if she could. Poldrian had *cheated* her!

Or maybe not. She *had* agreed to his price. She had not talked to any other wizards, or offered less money, she had only tried to delay part of the payment.

"But then she paid for it!" Lador said.

"She paid fifty, which would have been a tremendous bargain. The agreed-upon price was seventy-five, and she didn't pay *that*. Besides, turning her back is another spell. Twenty-five rounds of gold, and she'll be herself again. Not a great bargain, in my opinion."

"But...but..." her father spluttered.

"My master *tried* to talk her out of it, but she was determined — hard as stone, you might say."

"Why is she posed like that?" Kelder asked. "Did the wizard do that?"

"Not exactly," the apprentice replied. "She posed herself. Poldrian pretended he wanted to see whether she was beautiful enough to attract a rich idiot to pay what she owed, and she stood like that, and he cast the spell."

"He tricked her!"

"Well, he thought you'd rather have a pretty statue, not a miserable weepy one."

"We don't want a statue at all!"

"Well, you have one anyway. There's no point in yelling at *me*; I'm just an apprentice."

"Listen," Lador said, "if we could raise, say, *ten* rounds of gold, to make the sixty it should have been, would Poldrian turn her back?"

"I doubt it. A deal is a deal."

"Maybe we could find *another* wizard who can turn her back," her father said.

"That's entirely possible," the apprentice said. "My master would have no objection; he's made his point. But I don't think it will be a great deal cheaper. Good luck!"

And then she heard the familiar tinkle of the bell at her mother's shop, and Sharra realized she had been delivered to her parents. The thump that woke her had probably been her own weight hitting the floor.

"Listen, we need to start talking to wizards," her father said.

"Of course," Lador said. Then, after a brief pause, he added, "but she certainly is a beautiful statue."

"She was a beautiful girl," Kelder replied, "and I want my daughter back!"

CHAPTER NINE

It became obvious to Sharra over the next several days that no one knew she was still alive and able to hear – but then, why would they? *She* certainly hadn't expected it. She was a little surprised that apparently even Poldrian and his apprentice hadn't expected it, but that did seem to be the case. No one ever addressed her directly, and she heard several people make remarks she was fairly sure would not have been made had they known.

Her presence and situation meant that she was the subject of several conversations that she would never have been permitted to hear if the speakers had known she was still conscious; prompted by seeing her statue, people spoke of her with unexpected bluntness.

She had never realized how much her sisters disliked her, or just how much of a fool both her parents thought her. Everyone who knew her, friends and family alike, seemed to think the only surprise about Dulzan leaving her was how long it had taken him. No one had ever expected her to get him back, short of using a love spell.

Several people who had given her money came in to see what had become of her, and several of them suggested that since it was too late to prevent her petrifaction, perhaps they might get their money back.

Her parents and Lador pointed out that while it was too late to *prevent* it, they still hoped to *reverse* it, and would prefer to keep the money toward that goal.

Some accepted that, though not always with good grace. More than one, though, argued it had been a short-term loan, not a gift, and with no evidence to the contrary, Kirsha made full or partial refunds to those people who insisted.

She made them, however, out of her own money; apparently no one had yet discovered where Sharra had kept her trove.

Virtually everyone who came into the shop remarked on what a beautiful statue Sharra was; strangers seemed more likely to say so than were people she knew. Customers sometimes asked what the statue was doing there, and whether Kirsha answered, truthfully or otherwise, depended on her mood.

This clearly got on her nerves, though, and about a sixnight after the transformation – blind as she was, and insensitive to heat or cold, Sharra had some difficulty in keeping track of time – Kirsha said, "We have to ger her out of here."

"She's too heavy for me and Lador to lift," Kelder replied. "And I don't want to waste money hiring professionals the way Poldrian did; we *need* all our money if we're ever going to change her back!"

"And if we dropped her and she broke…" Lador began.

"All right!" Kirsha snapped, cutting him off. "But if you find a way, I would really prefer not to have to look at her every day."

If Dulzan ever came to see her, he never spoke, and no one called him by name.

And no one, Sharra noticed, ever said they missed her – not even her parents. In fact, more than one visitor said she was better company as a statue, or made some other similar rude comment.

Perhaps eight or nine days after she was petrified the doorbell jingled, and Lador's voice shouted, "I found one!"

"Found one what?" Kirsha demanded, obviously irritated.

"A wizard who can turn Aunt Sharra back!" Then, in a somewhat lower tone, he said, "Or at least she thinks she can. She says it depends exactly which spell Poldrian used; if it was something strange and obscure, maybe not. And there are irreversible petrifaction spells, but if Poldrian wasn't lying, and it can be undone, and it's not anything really rare, she says she can do it."

"Did you ask the price?"

There was a brief uncomfortable silence before Lador answered, "Well, that's the bad part."

"Go on."

"She wants thirty rounds of gold."

This time the pause was longer and obviously uncomfortable even to blind Sharra before Kirsha said, "And how is that any better than just paying Poldrian?"

"I didn't *agree* to that," Lador said. "I'm sure we can bargain her down. I thought maybe Grandfather should handle that part; he must have a lot of experience in bargaining."

"He can try. But I don't know."

"I'll keep looking. There are still many more wizards on Wizard Street, and maybe someone has a cheaper counter-spell."

A few days later the doorbell rang again, and after a brief round of greetings Lador said, "She can hear us."

"What?" Kirsha asked.

"Zarimol the Mage says that Aunt Sharra can probably hear us. He says that Poldrian probably used Fendel's Superior Petrifaction, which is the best of all the reversible ways to turn someone to stone, and that usually the victims of that spell remain sort of semi-conscious. They can't see or feel or smell anything, but they *can* still hear." Then, for the first time since her transformation, someone addressed her directly.

"If you can hear me, Aunt Sharra," Lador said, "we're still trying to find a way to turn you back. We've found a dozen wizards who say they can do it, but so far the absolute best price we've gotten is eighteen rounds of gold, and of course we don't have that much, and honestly, I'm not entirely sure he really can, but we talked one of the others down to twenty." He hesitated, then added, "We found your hoard, finally. Nine rounds. I've put it somewhere safe. With that, we're almost halfway there!"

"She can't hear you," Kirsha said angrily. "That wizard's making a joke. She's just a piece of stone!"

"Zarimol says her soul is still in there, or the spell wouldn't be reversible."

"I don't believe it. She's gone. Maybe there's a way to bring it back, or maybe that horrible Poldrian is just teasing us about that, but she's not there. Your Zarimol is being cruel, giving us false hope."

"I'm not going to argue, Grandmother, but I really don't think he is."

After that, as the months passed, every so often Lador would speak to her, to reassure her that she would be rescued someday. But he rarely had any news; the best offer they had found remained eighteen rounds, the best *trustworthy* offer was still twenty, and the available savings had not yet reached ten.

Sharra had no idea how long she had been stone when she heard her mother weeping, and gradually pieced together that her father had died. It was several days before Lador found a moment to explain that Kelder had collapsed without warning in Grandgate Market, and was gone before any sort of healer could reach him. Kirsha thought he had died of a broken heart, presumably over his youngest daughter's fate, but Lador thought it was just one of those things – a burst blood vessel, or a curse meant for someone else, or some other everyday mischance.

Sharra wished she could weep, but of course, she could not. Even if she had been taken to the field, she could not have seen her father's pyre.

She did wonder what people had said about him. She thought it would mostly be good things, that he had been respected and loved, but then, she had thought *she* was loved and admired, and now knew that wasn't the case.

Her mother gave up the shop not long thereafter, and moved in with Nerra, leaving Lador in charge of the weaving business, even though he had not yet qualified as a master weaver. He was at the highest rank of journeyman, but not yet a master.

Business was spotty after that, and Lador sometimes spent boring afternoons talking to his petrified aunt, rather than nonexistent customers. He never said so, but Sharra was fairly sure that he was not only not adding to the restoration fund, but sometimes borrowed from it to pay rent to his grandmother and to keep the business going; the total he quoted had stopped going up.

And then one day Lador came into the shop and said, "Aunt Sharra, you may be moving soon. I spoke to someone who collects statuary, and if he's willing to pay enough you'll be joining his collection. Just until we can get you turned back, of course! No one's selling you into slavery or anything. He'll be here this afternoon to get a look at you."

Sharra would have blinked, if she could. She had dozens of questions. Who was this person, and how was this supposed to work? Did this buyer *know* she was a real person, and not a sculptor's handiwork?

Lador did not volunteer any answers to her unasked questions; she thought she heard him go into the back room.

Some time later the doorbell rang again, and Lador greeted the new arrival with, "Welcome, my lord!"

Sharra heard shuffling feet and other sounds, and then a stranger's voice said, "This is the one, then?" He had a trace of an accent she could not place.

"Yes, Lord Landessin."

"That's chalcedony, isn't it? Very pretty shade, rather unusual."

"I...wouldn't know, my lord. I never spoke with the sculptor, and my grandfather never mentioned it."

"It's beautiful work. It would be perfect for my entrance hall."

"Then I hope we can agree on a price, my lord. My late grandfather bought it on a whim, and since his passing I haven't had any use for it."

Sharra marveled at how smoothly and easily Lador lied. She wished he had been that quick with his tongue when she had brought Sindel to the shop. And this Lord Landessin obviously did *not* know she had once been a living woman.

"Well, I am fairly certain I can take it off your hands. Would you consider, perhaps, five rounds of silver?"

Sharra felt insulted by the offer. She wished she could see Lador's face; she was sure he had expected far more. Not that either of them knew what statues sold for.

After a pause, Lador said, "I'm afraid that I can't consider that, no. I do have some idea what my grandfather paid for it, and while he may have been swindled, I cannot believe he was *that* far off. Shall we at least discuss the right metal for the coinage?"

"So you want gold."

"Yes, I do," Lador replied.

Lord Landessin sighed. "Very well, then; I agree it's worth four bits in gold."

"That's the same thing as five rounds of silver!"

"Is it? Oh, of course it is. All right, then, *five* bits."

"My lord, you are offending me. Make a serious offer!"

"What did your grandfather pay, then?"

"Twenty-five rounds!"

There was a moment of silence; then Lord Landessin said gently, "My dear boy, your grandfather most certainly *was* swindled!" After a few awkward seconds of silence, he said, "I could pay two."

"Twenty!"

The bargaining continued for a good half-hour, Sharra judged, before the two men finally settled on six and a half rounds. At least twice she had thought Lord Landessin was going to walk away, and she was not sure whether that would have been a good thing, or a bad one. While she did not particularly want to be sold and carried off somewhere, six and a half rounds would be a significant addition to Lador's savings and a step toward her eventual rescue.

She thought that Lador had probably gotten a good price. Either that, or Lord Landessin was a first-rate actor. She wished she could talk to Lador about the situation; this sale should bring the total to sixteen or seventeen rounds, if Lador hadn't pilfered too much, and she wondered whether he had any plans for raising the rest of the money. She also wondered how he intended to get her back once he did have the money – or would he bring the wizard to wherever Lord Landessin put her?

After she heard the door close, presumably indicating that Landessin had gone, she hoped Lador would talk to her and answer some of her questions. He did not. Instead she heard him muttering to himself, and then silence.

Hours later the door opened, and heavy footsteps surrounded her. She did not feel it – she never felt *anything* – but she was fairly certain she was being moved. She did not know how – ropes and pulleys, metal levers, raw muscle, or what – but by the sound of it, she was being moved out into the street and loaded into a cart or wagon.

Then she heard the creak of wheels, and knew she was on her way to wherever Lord Landessin intended to keep her. She tried to guess from passing sounds where she was going, but could not be sure.

But then she heard footsteps on planking, creaking wood, and splashing water, and she knew she was at a waterfront somewhere. She was, she realized, being loaded onto a ship. She was leaving Ethshar of the Sands.

She had never left the city before. She had never wanted to. She *really* didn't want to leave it *now*, since this was where Poldrian was, not to mention her less-than-loving family, but she was not offered a choice.

Then she heard sails flapping and snapping taut, sailors shouting, and she knew the ship was setting sail.

She had only the vaguest sense of time, so she was not sure how long she was at sea, but eventually there came a time when she could hear voices discussing their destination, now apparently in sight: Ethshar of the Spices.

She wondered whether Lador had known she would be taken out of Ethshar of the Sands when he sold her, or whether he knew *where* she would be taken.

Or whether he even cared. Maybe he had just wanted Lord Landessin's money – and her own.

They reached shore and she was taken off the ship and loaded into another wagon. She heard ordinary street noises for awhile and then a quieter area, and then much grunting and grumbling as she was carried into what she assumed was Lord Landessin's house.

There, as best she could judge, she was set on a pedestal or in a niche near the entrance. From the acoustics, she guessed she was in a large room with a hard floor – stone or tile, perhaps.

Then the men who had brought her left; she heard Lord Landessin paying their fee, and including "a little something extra" for doing their job so well. There were footsteps, the sound of a door closing, and then silence. She wondered whether she was alone.

But then Lord Landessin said, "Beautiful, just beautiful. If you really were carved, my dear, and not transformed, I hope my agents can find the sculptor who made you, so I can buy more such masterpieces! And if you were alive once and can hear me now, know that I have given you a place of honor in my home."

Sharra was shocked. He *knew* she might have been a real woman, and didn't seem to care. He certainly gave no indication that he intended to investigate further, or try to turn her back.

A place of honor in his home? Who cared about *that*? She wanted her life back!

If she ever was restored to life, she would have a few things to say to her nephew about selling her to this man.

CHAPTER TEN

Time passed. Sharra did not know how much time. She had no way of knowing how long any silence had lasted, or how long she had slept when she slept. She heard people go in and out of the room where she was displayed; she heard Lord Landessin speak with some of them. She heard him discuss other purchases for his collection of statuary.

Most of the people she heard had the same accent as Lord Landessin; she supposed it was the common speech of Ethshar of the Spices.

She heard him point her out to some of his visitors – or at least, she assumed it was her; apparently he had other statues of women in this room, as well. The responses were usually positive, praising her beauty, pronouncing her a magnificent piece of work – and they were always brief; a few seconds of admiration and the subject was done, the conversation moving on to something else.

None of them ever went into detail. No one mentioned a specific feature, such as her hands (she had always been proud of her delicate hands) or her eyes; it was always just a general comment or two on her beauty, and nothing more.

No one ever expressed any opinion on what the sculptor's model might have been like, or what the statue appeared to be thinking. No one ever suggested that she looked intelligent, or amusing, or anything other than beautiful.

And then there was the art critic who dismissed her as dismally unimaginative, saying that nothing about her – not her face, nor her pose, nor her expression – was in any way original. Lord Landessin seemed unsurprised by this response, and asked, "But isn't she lovely, all the same?"

"Oh, I suppose," the critic said. "But I want more from art than mere beauty."

Then the door closed, and if the conversation continued, she could not hear it.

It registered with Sharra fairly quickly that Lord Landessin did not seem to have a wife or a lover. He did have a sister who stopped by once or twice, but no other family was ever mentioned.

She wondered when, or if, Lador would ever carry through on his promise to save her.

As time dragged on, Sharra found herself remembering things – she had little else to do, and feared that she would go mad if she didn't do *something*. She tried to recall every detail of her childhood, of her marriage to Dulzan, of her entire life. She would come up with categories, and try to remember every event that fit in them – how many times in her life had she been scratched by a cat? How many times had she called her sisters names?

How many times had she done her sisters favors?

That one was depressing, because she realized that she could not think of a single instance when she had done anything nice for Dallisa or Nerra without expecting something in exchange. She did not always *get* something in exchange, but she had always expected it. After all, she was the youngest and prettiest of the three sisters; wasn't it just right and fair that the others should pamper her?

But maybe, she thought, it wasn't always.

In fact, they *had* pampered her when she was a little girl, but that had gradually faded away as she got older. It seemed as if the more she had *expected* her sisters to defer to her and give her whatever she wanted, the less willing they were to do so. When she was six and Nerra was eleven and Dallisa was thirteen, they had given her candy and handed down their old toys and had brushed out her hair without being asked; by the time *she* was eleven no one gave her treats, there were no more old toys to pass along, and the others were too busy doing their own hair and trying to impress boys to pay any attention to *her* appearance. She had thought that was completely unjust; why did getting older mean she was no longer entitled to their attention?

But then, decades later she had thought getting older was why she was no longer entitled to *Dulzan's* attention, and look where that had led her!

She stood helpless for what seemed like an impossibly long time, so long that her previous life began to feel like no more than a dream, and at one point it occurred to her that she was still beautiful, that she would *always* be beautiful as long as she remained a statue – and what good was it now? Beauty alone would not get her anything. It had not been enough to keep Dulzan. It had apparently not been enough to get Lador to rescue her. It had not prompted Lord Landessin to research her history.

One day brought a sudden change – unfamiliar voices, some shouting instructions, others hushed so that she could not make out their words. Magicians were coming and going, and other people as well, some familiar, some not.

At last she realized what was happening. Lord Landessin was dying. She was not sure of the cause – some illness, presumably. She heard someone say it was too late, that the witches should have been summoned sooner.

And then the tone changed, all urgency gone; everything slowed down, and Sharra knew that Lord Landessin was gone.

She heard some of the arrangements for his funeral; his pyre would be built in the garden behind the house. His sister would manage everything, and her four children would assist.

This was the first time Sharra had ever heard these children mentioned; apparently Lord Landessin had had three nephews and a niece. If any of them had ever passed through the room where Sharra stood, they had not said anything to identify themselves.

She did not know how she felt about this, or how she *should* feel about it. After all, she had never really met Lord Landessin. She had not known him beyond a voice and the fact that he collected statuary without worrying about its origins.

Dozens of low voices came and went the day of the funeral, but she could never make out enough of what was being said to identify anyone or make sense of what was happening.

Then there was quiet for a time – she estimated it at a few days, though she could not be sure – when so far as she could tell, no one came past her at all. When that ended she heard footsteps and various noises of objects being moved around, but no one said anything she could understand.

Then there was another long quiet period, which ended with footsteps and a man's voice proclaiming, "Oh, this is splendid!" He spoke just a little bit oddly, and she realized he did not have the accent of Ethshar of the Spices. It was not quite the accent of her home city, Ethshar of the Sands, either, but another slight variant on their common tongue.

"I hope you'll find it suitable," said a woman's voice. *She* had the now-familiar Spices accent.

"Well, we'll see. Are these statues included?"

"Oh, yes. We have no use for them."

"*All* of them? There must be dozens!"

"Hundreds. Our uncle collected statuary. We've already taken the ones we wanted – not that any of us share his passion for carved stone."

"Some of these are beautiful – that woman, for example." Sharra could not tell whether he meant her, or some other statue; she knew from previous overheard conversations that there were at least two or three others nearby.

She realized she did not actually *care* whether he meant her. It didn't matter whether strangers thought she was the most beautiful woman in the world, let alone best of the statues in the room.

"Uncle Landessin thought so," the woman said.

"And they're included in the rental terms you quoted me?"

"Oh, yes. That's easier than trying to find somewhere else to put them all."

"Hmm." There was a brief pause, and then the man said, "I suppose I could play the wealthy eccentric."

"Uncle Landessin *was* a wealthy eccentric."

"That's obvious. But I have customers I want to impress, and this place…"

"Do you have a large family, then? It's a very big house."

There was a bark of laughter. "My family's all back in Ethshar of the Rocks; it's just me and my staff."

"Then why…" The woman's voice cut off abruptly; Sharra supposed she had just realized she didn't want to say anything that might drive away a prospective tenant.

"I told you, I have customers I want to impress, and the price you offered – well, it's very tempting."

The woman sighed.

"Not many people looking to rent a place like this, are there?" the man asked.

"It's true. Most people looking for a place this big *buy* one, or build it."

"Which is why you aren't asking more."

"It's been standing empty for months; we didn't *start out* offering such a bargain."

"Well, let's see the rest of it, and then I'll decide if *I* think it's a bargain."

Footsteps receded, voices faded, and Sharra found herself hoping that the man *would* rent the place. She wanted to hear human voices again. She had existed in silent solitude for too long.

She wished that he had a big family with him; the sound of children playing would be wonderful, or teenage girls gossiping and laughing. Even if she couldn't join in, she yearned to hear normal conversation again. Maybe he would turn it down, and the next prospect would have a dozen kids.

But he didn't turn it down; he took it.

His name was Gror the Merchant, but judging by the conversations Sharra heard over the next year or two he could have called himself Gror the Smuggler with equal accuracy. He brought buyers and sellers to his new home fairly often; Sharra could not really judge time with any accuracy, but she thought he averaged a guest discussing business every sixnight or so. Most of them had foreign accents, and sometimes the conversations were in languages other than Ethsharitic, but the bits she overheard seemed to involve getting weapons from the forges of the Small Kingdoms to both sides of the ongoing civil war in Tintallion without drawing the attention of the overlords of Ethshar. Apparently the overlords didn't want armies of heavily-armed Tintallionese on their northwestern frontier. Sharra guessed they thought that the civil war couldn't last forever, though it had been going on for decades, and that once it was over the Tintallionese might want to direct those weapons elsewhere.

Some of these visitors mentioned the statuary, but as on Gror's initial arrival Sharra never knew, when they remarked on a statue's beauty, whether they meant her or one of the others.

There were other guests – all female, many prone to giggling, and some obviously drunk. Some of them stayed for days; others came and went in what Sharra estimated to be no more than a single night.

And there were two men who were apparently Gror's brothers who visited once in a while – not very often, though. The one named Bragen came perhaps a dozen times; Kargan less frequently. They only seemed to discuss business; if they ever spoke much about family or other concerns it did not happen where she could hear it.

Gror also had several servants who were around even when there were no guests, but Sharra was not sure just how many. She learned to recognize some of their voices, but not all; they did not speak very much around her, and she had the impression that some came and went, that not everyone Gror employed chose to stay.

The novelty of these new residents wore off quickly, and the tedium and loneliness grew ever harder to bear – but she had no choice. She was stone, unable to see or feel or move.

Since she could see nothing, and her surroundings were usually silent, she still had far too much time to think. She reviewed her life, over and over, and was dismayed by how few of those memories brought her any joy. All that time she had spent trying to make others admire her, and now she saw that no one ever really had. Some had admired her beauty, but none had ever admired *her*.

She remembered the fancy parties she had gone to, where she had tried to impress everyone with her beautiful clothes and Dulzan's talents and success, and she wondered whether anyone had really been impressed. She had thought they would all envy her, but did *anyone* really envy her?

She thought about all the faces she had seen over the years, and how they had reacted to her, from her sisters smiling at her when she was very young to Poldrian's disdainful expression as he cast the spell that turned her to stone. Had any of them ever looked impressed or envious?

She couldn't think of a single one who had. When she thought back and remembered their faces, their reactions, and what they said in response to her words, she realized that most of them had probably considered her a boor, boasting about nothing.

She had spent her entire life basically telling people, "Look at me!" without giving them any reason to *want* to. She had fought for social positions that did not, in the end, *mean* anything. She had been so very proud of visiting the overlord's palace without ever thinking of doing anything to deserve it. She had met dozens of people who worked in the palace, trying to make the city safer, richer, and better, and she had never once thought of doing anything to help any of them.

She remembered her supposed friends in Brightside and at the palace, the ones she had gossiped with, and realized she did not really know anything about most of them, and she didn't miss them. She missed her parents, and her sisters, and some of the friends she had known when she was young, and most of all she missed Dulzan.

She wished she had not driven him away. She knew that she had; it had not been her appearance that mattered, but her sharp tongue. If she had ever once tried to enjoy what he did, his friends at Tizzi's Tavern…

But she never had, and now it was too late.

Then one day, as she had been feeling particularly miserable, the silence was broken by a new voice exclaiming, "By the gods!"

"Impressive, isn't it?" Gror's voice responded.

"All these *statues*!"

"Lord Landessin collected them. The whole house is jammed with statuary of one sort or another."

"Who's Lord Landessin? A customer?"

"No, no. He's dead, I'm afraid, and I'm leasing this place from his estate. His heirs didn't want to live here, and there aren't too many people who want to rent something like this, so I got a good deal. Lord Landessin's collection came with it. It impresses some of my clients. Naturally, I don't tell *them* it all came with the house, or that I don't own the place. Actually, I have an arrangement with Landessin's heirs that if any of my customers take a fancy to any of the sculptures, I can negotiate a sale and keep a 25% commission."

"Where did he get them all?"

"His niece told me that he spent most of his life roaming around the World, buying every sculpture or carving he could. He had inherited a fortune, and held some position in the overlord's government that required extensive traveling; the niece was a little vague about the exact nature of her uncle's duties, but apparently he spent years at a time in the Small Kingdoms or the Baronies of Sardiron, and invariably returned home with dozens of new statues."

There was a slight pause before the new voice said, "Do you think he was a spy?"

"Probably nothing quite so crude as that, but I suspect he did indeed represent the Hegemony's interests in some clandestine way. Come on, lad, and I'll show you the rest of the house. You'll want to see where you'll be sleeping, I'm sure."

"Of course, Uncle. Lead the way!"

And then there were receding footsteps, and silence.

That was interesting; Sharra thought she might have just learned more about Lord Landessin in that brief conversation than she had in the years she stood there before he died. And that thing about Gror being able to sell the statuary – did that mean she might have a new owner someday? She hadn't heard anyone discuss such a possibility before.

And this new arrival was apparently Gror's nephew, Kargan's son. She hadn't known he had one.

Some time later – she still could not judge time with any accuracy – she heard footsteps approaching, and then she actually *felt* something, for the first time in years: a sharp pricking in her right forearm. It only lasted an instant, and then it was gone, and the footsteps moved away.

After so long feeling nothing at all, it had felt shockingly intense, as if a red-hot blade had plunged into her flesh, but she realized almost immediately that it had been no more than a pin-prick, at most. Still, she wanted to react, to jerk away, to blink in astonishment, to shout – but of course, she couldn't.

What *was* that? How could she have felt a touch? Could the enchantment have started to wear off? Or was this some *other* magic at work?

Maybe it was. Maybe whoever had walked up to her was a magician of some sort. But why would this magician be doing…whatever it was? Did the magician realize she wasn't just a statue?

Not very long after that there was a great deal of activity, and Sharra realized she was being moved, along with some of the other statues. This time there were no rumbling wheels or creaking timbers, so she did not think she was in a cart or on a ship. She could not figure out *how* she was being moved, but she could hear wind, and the noise of crowds in the streets, and then men shouting to one another as they directed each other in setting her into her new place – wherever it was.

And they were delivering other statues, as well. She could not tell how many.

A little later they were back, with more statues – and then again, and again.

Finally, though, everything was apparently in place, and silence descended again.

She wondered where she was, and who had bought her – and why had her new owner bought so *many* statues? Gror's 25% would probably make him rich!

But then, he had probably been rich already.

Some time later she heard two voices, one male, the other female. She thought the male voice sounded like Gror's nephew, though she wasn't certain; the female was unfamiliar. The two of them were talking somewhere not far away.

And then an odd thing happened. The male voice fell silent, and the female voice kept talking, but seemed to be carrying on just one side of a conversation. Then she spoke with maybe-Gror's-nephew again, apparently relaying what someone else had told her. The conversation sounded excited, but Sharra could not make out the words.

Then the voices moved a little closer and went through a similar, though shorter, exchange, and then another, and Sharra realized that the woman was talking to other statues – other people who had been turned to stone – and somehow getting answers, answers Sharra could not hear, which the woman was relaying to the nephew, whose name appeared to be Morvash.

Finally, the woman spoke loudly and clearly, from quite close, asking, "Who are you?"

Sharra could not speak, of course, but she thought, *I am Sharra the...the Charming*. She knew she had also unwillingly thought, *I am Sharra the Petty*, but hoped the woman hadn't sensed that.

"How did you come to be turned to stone? When did it happen?"

The whole story flashed through her thoughts – Dulzan's departure, her agreement with Poldrian, being unable to come up with the money, being petrified, Lador promising to help but instead selling her to Lord Landessin, all of it.

The woman said, presumably to Morvash, "She calls herself Sharra the Charming, though I get the impression not everyone called her that. Disputed a bill with a wizard named Poldrian. He warned her, but she didn't think he'd really do it. From what she heard, he did offer to turn her back for a fee, but her family declined. That was in Ethshar of the Sands about thirty years ago."

Then the two moved on, and the woman reported that the next statue was Abaran of Fishertown.

The voices gradually faded as they worked their way through more statues. Sharra did not concern herself with what they were saying, but only with what they had already said.

Thirty years. If that woman was right, she had been a statue for *thirty years*. What had happened to her family in all those years?

When they were gone silence descended once more, leaving Sharra to try to grasp that *thirty years* had passed, but not very long after that Gror's nephew, Morvash, came back and spoke directly to the statues.

"I'm Morvash of the Shadows," he said. "I'm a journeyman wizard. I know you're all people who were turned to stone, rather than real statues, and I'm looking for spells that can turn you back, but it may take quite some time to learn them. I know some of you can hear me, but I'm afraid I can't hear you at all. The woman who was here the other day who spoke to you is a witch by the name of Ariella, and she can hear some of your thoughts, at least sometimes—she couldn't hear all of you, just some. Whether this means the others were sleeping, or dead, or gone mad, we don't know. Anyway, we're working on rescuing you. Don't lose hope."

Those words swept over Sharra like a wave of joy; she was going to be human again!

But then reality set in. She was going to be human again *if* Morvash was telling the truth, and *if* he could learn the right spells, and *if* they worked correctly. There was no way of telling how long that might take. It could be years.

Still, there was a chance, a better chance than she had had at least since Lador sold her to Lord Landessin. It had long been obvious that Lador wasn't going to save her, but maybe this Morvash really would.

What *had* Lador done with the money he got for selling her? What had become of him – and of Dallisa, and Nerra, and Dulzan, and her mother? Had Lador died, perhaps? That would explain why no one had come to her rescue; probably no one else knew what had become of her.

Or maybe Lador was just an ungrateful little wretch.

Time passed, but she often heard Morvash's voice after that. Sometimes he was speaking to one or more of the statues; sometimes he was speaking to someone named Pender who seemed to be his apprentice or an assistant of some sort. Sharra hoped that Ariella might return, so that she could hold a real *conversation* for the first time in years, but it didn't happen.

Morvash did speak to her directly once, though.

"Sharra, isn't it? I tried to find the wizard who enchanted you, Poldrian of Morningside. He's still alive, but he won't get involved. He says he was done with the whole matter when he gave you back to your family, and he still won't turn you back unless he gets the rest of his money. He didn't know how to find your family anymore; he hadn't heard from them in years. I'm sorry I don't have better news."

Sharra wanted to scream at him, to give him the names of her family so they could be found, but she couldn't. Until Ariella came back, or Morvash succeeded in restoring her to human form, she couldn't tell him anything.

Her existence trapped in stone continued. Sometimes the knowledge that a wizard was trying to restore her to life was wonderfully cheering; other times she felt she might go mad with frustration that he had not succeeded yet. She heard Morvash and Pender talking and things bumping around, but nothing significant changed. Sometimes Morvash would offer messages of encouragement, but never any details on how his research was progressing.

And then at last Ariella was back briefly, interviewing the statues, assuring them that Morvash was almost ready to start trying out his spells on them. Sharra tried to tell her about her family, and the witch repeated some of the names back, but said, "I'm not sure whether there's any point in trying to contact them right now; let's wait and see whether the restoration spell works. Morvash is going to try it out on Prince Marek first, and see how that goes."

But...but... Sharra thought, but Ariella had moved on.

Then the witch was gone, and Sharra could do nothing but wait.

Now that the possibility of rescue seemed close she grew ever more desperate. She *needed* to get back to Crafton and see what had become of her family. She needed to get back to her old life, as soon as she could!

Ariella had given her the impression that Morvash would be trying his spell immediately, but she could hear no sign of it. Oh, there were some thumps and rattles, and she could hear Morvash and Pender speaking to each other, but that was all.

And then even those stopped, and everything was silent, and Sharra, as usual, had no idea what was going on.

Time passed – hours? Days? Years? She could not be sure, but she thought it was a day or two. Then Morvash and Pender were back, moving around again. Pender fell silent – or perhaps he went away, she couldn't tell.

Morvash, though, was muttering to himself occasionally, and then he started a chant. Was that the restoration spell? Even if it was, though, Ariella had said he would be trying it on some prince. Even if it worked, he might not get around to the rest of the statues for sixnights.

The chant seemed to go on forever – until it didn't.

But Sharra scarcely noticed that it had stopped; she was too distracted by being able to *see*. She could smell some sort of burning herb, she could feel her feet on a wooden floor, and she could *see*. She was in a long gallery, facing tall windows; sunlight was pouring in, filling the world with glorious color, and there were people all around her, a bizarre assortment of people who were looking about in astonishment.

She was human again. She was *alive* again!

CHAPTER ELEVEN

People were shouting and laughing and running about, but Sharra stood where she was, looking around, trying to identify Morvash. Someone in a wizard's robe was in an alcove at one end of the gallery, standing beside a naked couple and looking through an open door. Then another man in a wizard's robe stepped through the door—was *that* Morvash, perhaps?

The two wizards spoke, but she could not make out any of their conversation over the babble around her. The chatter was starting to fade, though, as everyone tried to take in their situation. Several of them were watching the two wizards.

Then the wizard who had been in the alcove originally turned and walked out into the gallery, looking around, still talking. The other wizard, a tall thin man in a dark blue robe, followed, continuing their conversation.

Then the shorter wizard raised his arms and shouted, "May I have your attention, please? Everyone?"

The remaining chatter faded away completely, and the wizard spoke into the silence.

"Forgive me if I repeat things you already know," he shouted, "but not all of you responded to attempts to communicate, so I can't be certain who knows what. Bear with me. I am Morvash of the Shadows, a wizard, originally from Ethshar of the Rocks but sent to live with my uncle in Ethshar of the Spices. Some of you may know the city by its older name, Azrad's Ethshar; some of you may not know it at all. Some of you may not understand a word I'm saying; we'll arrange for translations later.

"All of you were turned to stone, by one spell or another, and wound up in the collection of a wealthy nobleman named Lord Landessin, who was obsessed with sculpture and statuary. When Lord Landessin died his heirs rented his estate to my uncle, which was where I found you and realized you had been transformed, rather than carved. I took it upon myself to learn enough magic to turn you back. My uncle, understandably, did not want me conducting dangerous magical experiments in his home, so I rented this house and brought you all here.

"And now, much more quickly and thoroughly than I expected, here you are – a spell I intended to rescue just two of you has misfired, and instead brought *all* of you back to life at once.

"Today is the 26th day of the month of Leafcolor in the Year of Human Speech 5238. You are in the upstairs gallery of a wizard's house on Old East Avenue, near the southern boundary of the district known as the New City, not far from Southmarket and Arena.

"I do not know what has become of your homes or families or possessions; I had not yet taken the time to do any research about these matters.

"You are not prisoners. If you feel you are ready to deal with the World of the present day, you are free to go; my assistant Pender will show you to the door."

He paused, looking around, then said, "Just a moment." He strode through the crowd and out a doorway, and then Sharra heard him call, "Pender! Where are you?"

Sharra was not sure she heard a reply, but Morvash apparently did; he continued, "Well, get up here! I need help!"

A moment later Morvash and another man stepped into the gallery – and when the other man saw the tall wizard he suddenly fell to his knees and shouted something in a language Sharra could not understand.

In fact, Sharra did not understand much of what was going on around her, and she didn't really care. She was free at last, and she wanted to go *home*, to see her family again. These wizards, and all these other people, didn't have anything to do with her. Morvash had said she could go, and that was exactly what she intended to do. If Morvash had told the truth about the date she had been a statue for a little over *thirty years*; she *needed* to get home and see what had become of everyone she knew.

She particularly wanted to know what had become of Lador, and why he had never in thirty years carried through on his promise to rescue her. And what had become of Dulzan without her?

The kneeling man and the tall wizard were babbling at each other in that strange language while everyone else just watched; Sharra looked around, and thought most of them were just as baffled as she was. One or two did seem to be following the words, but perhaps they were merely pretending.

It didn't matter; she needed to get home. Morvash had said they were in Ethshar of the Spices; she needed to get back to Ethshar of the Sands.

Then the tall wizard looked up and spoke in Ethsharitic. "It seems I have important matters to attend to elsewhere. There is no rush about removing these people after all. I trust, though, that they will all be gone before I return."

Sharra did not bother to listen any further. Morvash had said that Pender would show her where the door was; which of these people was Pender?

Then the tall wizard marched out the door, and the kneeling man leapt to his feet and followed, saying something apologetic to Morvash on his way out.

Morvash announced, "It would appear I have lost my assistant. Did anyone here recognize the language they were speaking, and understand what was said?"

Someone raised a hand, and Morvash beckoned to him.

"They were speaking Sardironese," the man said. He proceeded to explain what had been said, but Sharra didn't listen. It didn't concern her.

But at last, Morvash addressed the entire group again. "Well, if anyone would like to leave now, and fend for himself, I will show you to the door. Those who would prefer to take a little more time, and receive what assistance I can provide in adapting to your new surroundings, please wait here; I'll be right back. Now, who's ready to go?"

Sharra stepped forward immediately. She was joined by three men in uniforms much like those the city guards wore, and two other women.

One of the women was wearing next to nothing, just a flimsy dancing costume of some sort, far more revealing than Sharra's own daring attire, and Morvash took her aside. He asked her something, and judging by her response she did not speak Ethsharitic. Sharra wondered whether perhaps the wizard wanted to keep her for himself. At any rate, after some discussion he turned her over to a big, strong young man who did not, in Sharra's opinion, look very bright. This man held the young woman's arm while the rest of the group proceeded through the doorway and down a hallway to the top of the stairs.

Along the way the three men in uniform discussed their situation; apparently they had been petrified for more than a century. One of them turned back, so there were only four former statues following Morvash. He paused when they reach the stairs and asked Sharra, "What about you?"

"I'm going home," Sharra replied firmly. "I'm not like these others; it's only been thirty years. Even if my husband is gone, my nephew will still be there." She hoped that was true.

"How will you get back, though? It's a long way to Ethshar of the Sands."

"I'll find a way. Come on!"

"All right," Morvash said. Then he asked the other woman whether she was sure she wanted to go, and she said she was.

At the foot of the stairs a bunch of animated furniture was wandering about; Sharra resisted the temptation to stare. A door stood wide open. Morvash cleared the way, and Sharra and the others marched down the steps to the street.

Morvash stayed in the house, and closed the door behind them.

The two men promptly turned right; they clearly knew where they were going. The woman seemed less certain, but then turned up a palm and followed them.

"Wait!" Sharra called, looking around. She had no idea where she was. The position of the sun meant it was not far from midday, but she could not tell whether it was before or after, so she could not determine directions.

The two men paused politely.

"Where can I get a ship to Ethshar of the Sands?" she asked.

"If it hasn't changed since the wizard enchanted us, Shiphaven," one of them said, pointing across the street.

"How do I get there?"

"Go down Canal Avenue to the overlord's palace," the other man said. "Then turn left and go out North Street."

"If it hasn't changed," the first one added.

"Thank you!" She turned. "Is that Canal Avenue?" she asked, pointing at the next cross-street.

"Yes."

She nodded, and set out in the direction indicated.

The walk was not a comfortable one. She had never been in Ethshar of the Spices before – or rather, she had never been flesh in this city – so she was not expecting to see anything she recognized, but it was still disconcerting to see the unfamiliar architecture and the clothes these people were wearing. Obviously, fashions had changed while she was a statue. Tunics were still standard attire, but they were cut differently than any she had ever seen before, with nipped-in waists and flared sleeves. Most of the men wore breeches, rather than kilts; when she had last been able to see, kilts had been more common. Women's skirts were not as full as she remembered.

It was also disconcerting how people *stared* at her. Was it because of her clothing? If so, was it because it was so old-fashioned, or because it was so immodest? Or were they just staring at her because she was a beautiful woman in a revealing dress?

She wondered whether people had stared at her when she was a statue.

The street under her feet seemed harder than she remembered, and her shoes were not really suited to it. Was that a difference between Ethshar of the Sands and Ethshar of the Spices, perhaps? Or was she simply not accustomed to walking anymore? After all, it had been thirty years.

Thirty years! That was hard to comprehend. How many of the people she knew back in Ethshar of the Sands were still alive? What would they be like?

She knew her father was dead, but was her mother all right? What had become of Dulzan, without her there to look after him? What had Lador been doing all this time, or her sisters? What had become of her money? What had happened to Poldrian?

She would find out, just as soon as she could.

She wished that man had given her some hint of how *far* it was to the overlord's palace, or how to recognize it when she saw it. She had assumed it would not be far at all, and that the palace would be obvious – the one in Ethshar of the Sands certainly was, with its immense central dome and the four side-vaults, but she could not see anything like that ahead. She crested a hill about two long blocks from Morvash's door, and the street beyond seemed to go on forever, straight down a long slope, with no dome anywhere in sight.

She walked on down the hill, past any number of large, elegant houses, but none of them really seemed like an overlord's palace.

At last, though, after a quarter of a mile or more, she could see a canal ahead, and a large yellow brick building beyond the canal that could be a palace. She certainly hoped that was it; her feet were beginning to get sore, and she felt a pang that she only recognized after some thought as hunger. She had forgotten what hunger felt like. She had likewise half forgotten thirst, and pain, and every other normal, natural sensation. The sun on her shoulders, the breeze on her face, the light and color she saw everywhere, the smells of sweat and smoke and spices all seemed new and strange, but pleasant; even pain and hunger were enjoyable simply because they were so novel after so long.

And the sounds! She had been able to hear as a statue, but she had spent all that time indoors, and the streets were awash in sounds she had almost forgotten – talking and shouting and laughter, doors slamming and wheels creaking.

Another quarter mile brought her to the edge of the canal, across from one end of that yellow brick building. That *had* to be the overlord's palace, though it looked nothing at all like the magnificent domed structure back in her home city.

She turned left, following the directions she had been given, walking alongside the canal, but after a short block the street ended, forcing her to turn left again – she could not go straight, turning right would drop her into the canal, and she was not about to turn back. After another short block, no more than a hundred feet, she came to another intersection and paused, trying to decide what to do. Going straight would be heading back the way she had come, and going left again would be going in a circle, so she turned right, thinking perhaps her guide had meant for her to turn left sooner than she had.

Or perhaps things had changed in the century since *he* was petrified. Maybe that wall blocking the street by the canal hadn't been there a hundred years ago. She turned right.

And one more short block brought her to a broad stone-paved plaza, bounded by the canal on her right. A stone bridge midway along that side of the square led across the canal to the palace.

She walked the length of the plaza, and found herself at a corner where no fewer than three streets led out of the square. Which of them was North Street – if any?

This was so *confusing*! She had not expected finding a ship back home to be so difficult!

She waved to a man passing by. "Excuse me," she called. "Which of these is North Street?"

He started, and stared at her for a moment before pointing. "That one," he said, pointing at the rightmost of the three. "The one that goes north."

"Is that north?"

"Well…not really, no. It's west." He pointed along the side of the plaza, toward the canal. "*That's* north. But North Street turns at the end of the palace canal and goes *almost* north."

"And that will get me to Shiphaven?"

"Well…it will get you to Spicetown, anyway."

"But I want to get to Shiphaven! I need to find a ship bound for Ethshar of the Sands."

"You can probably find a ship in Spicetown."

"But…" Sharra stopped and frowned. "Spicetown" did not sound like somewhere to find ships, but this city was the center of the entire World's spice trade, so maybe he was right.

The man hesitated, as if debating whether to say something.

"If I want to get to Shiphaven, how do I do it?" she asked.

The man looked up North Street, considering. "Well," he said, "if you go down here and turn left on Moat Street, then take the left-hand fork onto Warehouse Street past the Upper Canal and follow it around to Canalside Market and then out New Canal Street…"

"Never mind," Sharra said. She knew that even if those directions were accurate, she would never be able to remember and follow them. "Just tell me where I can find the waterfront."

"That way," the man said, pointing in the direction he had indicated as north. "A half-mile or so that way."

"Isn't the ocean to the south?"

"Ethshar isn't *on* the ocean. It's on the Gulf of the East, on the north side of the peninsula."

Geography outside her own city's walls had never been anything Sharra really paid much attention to, but that did sound vaguely familiar. "So if I go that way, I'll get to the waterfront eventually?"

"Yes. Um…if you don't mind my asking, where are you *from*?"

"Brightside, in Ethshar of the Sands." The habit of naming Brightside and omitting any mention of her humble origins in Crafton had survived her years as a statue, she realized; it had come out automatically, without a second's thought.

"How did you get *here*, without knowing any of this?"

Sharra did not want to waste time explaining her entire history, and boiled it down to the essentials. "I was kidnaped," she said.

"What?" The man looked shocked. "Do you want me to call a guardsman?"

"No, no." She waved a hand. "I'm fine. I was rescued. Now I just want to go home."

"Um…" He glanced around. "Are you sure you don't need any help? I could walk you to the docks."

That, Sharra thought, would be useful – but why was this person offering to go half a mile out of his way for a stranger?

A beautiful, scantily clad stranger from another city, who did not appear to have any friends or family who would notice if she went missing.

Maybe she wanted a guardsman after all – but no. Even without her husband, she could take care of herself.

"I'll be fine," she said.

"You know slavers hang around the docks, right?"

"Oh." This was getting so *complicated*. Maybe she should have waited for Morvash to arrange something after all, but she hadn't expected it to be difficult. She had thought she could just walk a few blocks to the docks and get on a ship. "I just want to go *home*," she said.

"To Ethshar of the Sands?"

"Yes!"

"By ship?"

"I don't care how!"

"Well, you could go by road. Just go up Merchant Street, then go right at the fork onto High Street, and that will take you straight to Westgate." He pointed at the middle road of the three.

"How far is it?"

"To Westgate? About a mile and a half."

"No, to Ethshar of the Sands."

"Oh. I'm not sure – maybe fifty leagues?"

"Fifty *leagues*?"

"Something like that."

"Oh, by… Never mind." She turned away and marched up North Street.

The man stood and watched her go, but then she heard his voice again.

"Wait!" he said, and she heard his running footsteps coming after her.

CHAPTER TWELVE

"Go away," she said, as he caught up to her.

"No, let me help," he said, walking beside her. "I won't touch you, I promise – at least, not unless you want me to." Then he shook his head. "No, not even then. I'm happily married. But I can't let someone as young and pretty as you wander about the streets alone dressed like that, not when you don't know your way around."

"I'll be fine. I'm not as young as I look." She grimaced to herself; she certainly wasn't, by perhaps fifty years in all.

"But…listen, I don't know what Ethshar of the Sands is like, but Ethshar of the Spices can be a dangerous place. There are slavers and thieves and pimps – you said you already got kidnaped once, so you should *know* it's not safe!"

"I was kidnaped back in Ethshar of the Sands, not here. This is just where I was brought." She glanced at him. He appeared genuinely concerned. "Don't you have your own business to attend to?"

"I was just on my way to Silk Street to see about some draperies; it can wait."

She looked around; there were a few dozen pedestrians in sight, and at least two ox-drawn wagons. If he tried to do anything she didn't like, a scream should bring help.

"All right," she said. "Where can I find passage back home?"

He glanced up North Street. "Well, I don't really know, to be honest, but I'd have thought Traders' Wharf in Newmarket would have been the best place to look, not on this side of the city at all."

Sharra stopped dead in her tracks and closed her eyes, then immediately opened them again; she had gone quite long enough in the dark already. She wondered whether the man who gave her directions was an idiot, or whether the city had changed since he was petrified. It *had* been a century, after all…

She really *should* have stayed with Morvash a little longer – but she was here now, and she wasn't eager to go back. She had already walked *this* far.

"All right," she said. "Where is the *closest* place I might find a ship to Ethshar of the Sands?"

"Well, if you just bear right at every fork from here, you'll come out alongside the Grand Canal, and you can follow it out to the Gulf. Ships dock all along it. But I don't know whether any of them go to Ethshar of the Sands."

"Thank you." She started walking again.

Once again, the man walked with her. "My name is Kordis of the Old City," he said. "What's yours?"

"Sharra," she replied.

He waited for a cognomen, but she did not say anything more, and when he realized she was not going to he asked, "You were really kidnaped?"

"Yes." She was still not sure whether he was genuinely just trying to help, or whether he had an ulterior motive, so she did not want to get into a conversation.

"You said you were rescued?"

"Yes."

"Who rescued you?"

"A wizard named Morvash of the Shadows."

"I never heard of him."

"Neither did I, until he freed me." That was not literally true, but it was close enough.

"So did he give you the money to get home? I assume the kidnappers robbed you of whatever you had."

"No, he didn't give…" She stopped again.

She could not *believe* she had not thought about this sooner. How could she have been so *stupid*? She had no money, not a single copper bit. All her carefully hoarded money, if it was still hers at all, was back in Ethshar of the Sands. She had hidden it in her parents' home, but of course that was thirty years ago, and anyway Lador had found it, and there was no knowing what had become of it by now.

Kordis stopped as well, and looked at her with a concerned expression.

"I don't have any money," she said. "It's all back in Ethshar of the Sands."

Kordis blinked at her. "Then how were you going to pay for your passage? If you were planning to pay on arrival – well, ship captains aren't usually very trusting. Do you have friends here you could borrow it from?"

"No, I don't," she admitted. "I'll need to earn it somehow." After what had happened back in Harvest of 5208 she was not about to try stealing it, or borrowing it, since she didn't know anyone here, or seducing some man into giving it to her.

But she did know *one* person here, more or less. She looked at Kordis, and conjured up her best wheedling tone. "Unless *you* could lend it to me? I promise I'll repay you once I get home." She gave him a smile that had gotten her any number of favors and gifts in her girlhood – her *first* girlhood.

"Oh, I can't afford that. I'm just a draper. I'm already operating on credit more than I like."

The smile vanished. "Then what am I going to *do*?" she asked, pretending to hold back tears – and then realizing that she was not pretending at all. Emotions she had not felt for thirty years were flooding back, now that she was once again flesh rather than stone.

"Is there someone you can send a message? Someone who could loan you money?"

"My nephew Lador – he owes me a lot of money, in fact." All the money Lord Landessin had paid Lador was rightfully hers, after all, as well as her own money that he had probably taken. "But he couldn't get it to me for days, maybe sixnights."

"Your *nephew*?" Kordis blinked again, then shook off his surprise.

"My older sister's son," she explained – not that that was *all* of the explanation, by any means.

After a pause, she added, "I would need somewhere to stay until he can send it." She looked pleadingly at Kordis.

"You think…oh, no! I think I may have given you the wrong impression. I have a wife, as I said, and we only have a single room – well, and my shop, but you can't…no. Just no."

Startled, Sharra realized that he had apparently been offering to help her entirely out of genuine concern, and not lust. She had not expected that; she had assumed he would be eager to have her sleeping in his home. "Then do you know somewhere I could go?"

He shook his head. "No, I'm afraid I don't."

"I can't sleep in your shop?"

"No."

The flat refusal surprised her, but from his tone she did not think there was any point in arguing. She frowned.

"It's not just *my* shop, you see. I share it with three others. You wouldn't be safe there."

"Oh." That seemed all too believable. She tried to think what other options she had. She had no friends or family in this city, no one she could stay with or borrow from. She could not steal the money she needed; she had no weapons or tools, and was too small to force anyone to give her anything, and in any case had no idea how to go about thieving.

She really would have to *earn* the money – but she had never in her life earned money. She had always had everything she needed given to her, by her parents or her sisters or Dulzan or her friends.

"You *will* need to earn your money, I guess," Kordis said, echoing her thoughts. "What skills do you have?"

Sharra was asking herself that same question. "I can cook, I suppose. Though not especially well." Dulzan had always been polite about the meals she prepared, but any time they had company she had hired a professional cook; she knew she hadn't been very good at it.

Kordis frowned.

"I was apprenticed to a weaver, but I didn't complete my apprenticeship. And that was a long time ago; I don't think I remember most of it."

"A long time ago? Then you didn't get very far?"

Sharra started to protest that she had served her parents for the full six years, even if she didn't finish, but then she remembered she looked eighteen or nineteen again, and even to a teenager, "a long time" would mean at least a few years. "Maybe not *that* long," she said. "But I really am older than I look."

"Well, I wouldn't know how to get started as a weaver…" Kordis began.

Sharra interrupted him. "I can't," she said. "I would need a journeyman's certificate before anyone would trust me, and I don't have one, and I'd need money to buy a loom and rent a shop if I wanted to start my own business, and I don't have it."

"You can't work in someone else's shop?"

"Not without being certified as a journeyman. I'm too old to start a new apprenticeship."

"I suppose that's true." He looked down at the dirt of the street, not meeting her eyes, and said, "There's one possibility; you're a beautiful girl…"

Sharra had known this was coming. "I really hope it won't come to that," she said. "There must be something else."

"Perhaps you could find a wealthy patron…"

Sharra looked around. They were standing at a four-way intersection, surrounded by shops, warehouses, people, and ox-drawn wagons. "Not here," she said. "I went through some much nicer neighborhoods earlier, though." She was not optimistic about the idea anywhere, though; she had tried that back in Brightside, when she was trying to raise money to pay Poldrian, and it hadn't worked. It was much harder than she had expected.

She wondered whether she should go back to Morvash's place after all; even if Morvash was no longer offering aid, that had seemed a much safer, wealthier area than this one.

Kordis cleared his throat. "I hesitate to suggest it, but perhaps you could convince a sea captain to take you back to your home for considerations other than money."

"Perhaps I could," Sharra agreed. "I'm not a blushing innocent, but I…I was married, and I was faithful to my husband…"

"You were *married*?"

"I keep telling you, I'm older than I look!" she snapped. Then she sighed, and looked around.

They were surrounded by people going about their business – wagon drivers hauling goods, workmen carrying their tools, men and women with sacks slung over their shoulders. It occurred to Sharra that while many of these people were obviously tradesmen, others did not appear to have any special skills or training. Some of them were talking and laughing together.

"Where do you think those people are going?" she asked, pointing at one group of large men.

Kordis followed her finger and said, "I don't know, but if you want a guess, they're on their way to the docks. There's decent money to be had loading and unloading ships."

"Could I work loading ships, maybe?"

Kordis looked at the men in coarse homespun, then at the delicate young woman in the revealing dress. "I don't think so," he said. "How much can you lift?"

"Oh." Her shoulders sagged. Now that he had said that, she could see the absurdity of the idea. A return to Morvash was looking more and more like her best option, but she had come this far, and going back would feel like a retreat. She wanted to solve a problem by herself for once, without relying on anyone else. She looked up first one street, then another, and up the street to her right a signboard caught her eye.

"What's that?" she asked.

Kordis looked where she was pointing. "The Winking Maiden? It's an inn, of course."

An inn? She had feared it was a brothel, but she would have expected a brothel's sign to emphasize other parts of the female anatomy; this sign showed a woman's face, smiling broadly with one eye closed. She had thought it might involve some sort of performance – she was at best only a passable singer, but she had been complimented on her dancing more than once, long ago, and she was willing to learn. Still, an inn might be just as good.

Sharra realized that she was about to suggest something she would have considered unthinkable all through her unfinished apprenticeship and the twenty years of her marriage to Dulzan, but now everything had changed. Whether she wanted to admit it or not, that marriage had ended thirty years ago, and her experiences since then had altered her outlook. Living in her parents' home again, begging her friends for money to pay Poldrian, and all those years as an ornament in Lord Landessin's mansion had driven much of the arrogance out of her.

"Do you think they might hire me as a serving girl?"

Kordis cocked his head to one side. "They might," he said.

Sharra started toward the inn, but Kordis hurried to catch up to her. "Serving girls aren't paid much," he said. "It might take years to save enough for passage to Ethshar of the Sands."

"It might," Sharra admitted, "but I'd have a roof over my head and enough to eat, which is more than I have now."

"Some patrons can be unruly."

"I can take care of myself.

She hoped that was true. She picked up her pace, Kordis still following.

CHAPTER THIRTEEN

The Winking Maiden was not hiring, though the innkeeper's behavior made it clear that he regretted that; he stared at Sharra, only occasionally remembering to look at her face.

"I'd need to fire one of my other girls," he said. "It wouldn't be fair. They're all family of one sort or another." He glanced at the back of the woman leaning against the wall by the hearth. "I could ask if any of them would like to quit…"

"No, that's all right," Sharra said. She was disappointed that she was not going to be hired immediately, but the man's reaction made it obvious that she could expect to find work *somewhere*.

In fact, it was at the third inn she tried, the Crooked Mast, that she was hired. It was an ancient wooden structure overlooking the Grand Canal, looking rather as if it might fall into the water at any moment.

"Purely on a trial basis, you understand," the innkeeper said. "If you spill drinks or make a mess or can't keep up, you'll be out in a sixnight."

"I understand," Sharra told her.

"The pay is room, board, and two bits a day; you work from midday to midnight. With a face like yours you'll probably pick up a few extra coins here and there, and it won't hurt my feelings if you choose to share them."

Sharra smiled wryly. "Of course," she said.

"And you'll need proper clothing, a tunic and skirt and apron."

Sharra looked down at herself. "Could you loan me those? Or one of the other girls? All I have is what you see."

"You'll have to arrange that yourself. I can't spare anything that would fit you."

She nodded.

When the details were settled Kordis took her aside and asked, "Are you sure about this?"

"I think it's the best I can do," Sharra said. She hesitated, then grabbed him in an embrace and kissed his cheek. It felt wonderful to touch another human being after so long. "Thank you for your help," she said. "Your wife is a fortunate woman."

Kordis flushed slightly and pulled away. "May the gods be kind to you, Sharra of the Sands."

"And to you, Kordis of the Old City."

Then she watched as he slipped out the door of the inn into the busy street.

The innkeeper had watched this silently; now she said, "I want you to be ready for the suppertime rush tonight; go upstairs and see whether anyone can loan you a tunic."

Sharra hurried to obey.

Most of the inn's staff slept in the third-floor attic; the only furniture consisted of three mattresses, and an assortment of boxes and chests surrounding two of the mattresses. The third lay bare and alone in one corner.

A woman was sitting on one of the mattresses, playing a plaintive tune on a wooden flute; she looked up when Sharra's head appeared in the stairwell, set the flute down, and watched the new arrival.

"Hello," Sharra said.

The other woman didn't respond.

"My name is Sharra the..," Sharra began. Then she stopped, and reconsidered. She had intended to say "Sharra the Charming," but she realized she did not want to call herself that anymore. She had had thirty years to think about it, and had long ago realized that it was a stupid, childish name to give herself, and no one else had ever actually called her that and meant it. She remembered what Kordis had called her, and concluded, "Sharra of the Sands."

"I'm Irith. Virina hired you to take Lissa's place?"

Sharra glanced at the empty mattress. "I suppose so," she said.

"Then you sleep there," Irith said, jerking a thumb. "Put your stuff anywhere it fits."

"I don't *have* any stuff."

Irith frowned. "Why not?"

"I was robbed," Sharra said. "I'm taking this job to make enough money to get home."

"Why are you dressed like that?"

"It's what I was wearing when…when the robbers caught me."

"Why? I mean, why were you dressed like that?"

"I was trying to impress someone. It didn't work." She hesitated, looking down at her dress, then asked, "Would you have a spare tunic I might borrow? I'll return it as soon as I can get my own."

Irith considered Sharra for a moment, then said, "You'll need a skirt, too. And an apron. And I don't think those shoes are going to last very long. You're going to be on your feet all day."

Sharra grimaced. "I thought I could just put a tunic over the dress for now."

Irith snorted. "You do know there's a slit up one side of your skirt, don't you?"

"Of course I do!"

"And about every third customer is going to try to slip his hand in there."

"Oh." Sharra looked down again, judged where tabletop height would be, and decided Irith was probably right.

"Of course, if you don't *mind* that…" Irith said.

"I mind," Sharra said. "But I don't have any money for new clothes. This dress is literally all I have right now. Please, could you loan me a tunic?"

"Where'd you get a dress like that, anyway? Did you make it?"

"No. I couldn't make anything like this."

"You bought it?"

Sharra hesitated, then admitted, "My sister made it for me."

"Was it for something special?"

She was not about to admit the truth, that she had hoped to sway a wizard into forgiving a debt; she substituted, "I just wanted to look nice."

"You said you wanted to impress someone. Trying to catch a rich husband?"

"No, I *had* a husband. I was just showing off." That was why she had bought dresses on Luxury Street often enough, even if this wasn't one of them. She knew that before Dulzan left her she would never have admitted that, but thirty years of introspection had had an effect.

"You were married? What happened?"

"He left me."

"With *your* looks?"

Sharra grimaced. "I was…" She groped for the right word. She knew that she had been known as Sharra the Petty, but "petty" didn't really seem to convey it. "I did not treat him well," she said.

She saw the change in Irith's expression, and hastily said, "That was a long time ago."

"Really? How old were you when you married him, twelve?"

"Eighteen. I'm older than I look." She was getting tired of saying that.

"You must be. *You* didn't treat *him* well?"

Sharra did not answer that.

"Did *he* treat *you* well, before he left?"

"Better than I deserved," Sharra said.

It would have taken so little, she thought, to have kept Dulzan reasonably happy. If she had let him spend his time at Tizzi's Tavern with his friends, if she hadn't dragged him to those fancy events at the overlord's palace…

Irith looked unconvinced, but she turned to a battered wooden chest and lifted the lid. "I only have the two, the one I'm wearing and this one, so try not to damage it." She lifted out a folded white tunic.

"Thank you!" Sharra said, stepping forward.

Irith hesitated. "Seriously, this is just a loan until you can get your own."

"I understand that. I'll return it as soon as I can."

Reluctantly, Irith gave her the tunic; Sharra accepted it, and asked, "Do you have a skirt to go with it?"

"I'm not sure how well it will fit," Irith said, as she rummaged through the chest. "I'm taller than you are."

"I can fold over the waistband."

"I suppose." Irith pulled out a skirt of dull brown wool, poorly cut, badly woven, and lacking any sort of decoration. Sharra bit her lip; that would be the ugliest thing she had ever worn in her *life*. Still, it would do. She accepted the skirt, and set it aside while she began tugging at the shoulders of her gown. She had been wearing that thing for thirty years, and would be happy to be rid of it.

Irith watched as Sharra stripped off her dress and pulled the tunic over her head. Both women noticed it was a little baggy, but neither remarked on it.

Sharra stepped into the skirt and pulled it up, but discovered when she buttoned it that it did not want to stay at her waist; it slid down to her hips and she had the definite impression that it might fall to the floor if she let it go. She looked for a drawstring, but found none. "Do you have a belt I could use?" she asked.

"No. You'll need to find a bit of rope. Virina probably has something."

Sharra grimaced. "What about an apron?"

"No." Irith nodded toward the other mattress. "Challin might have one. She's working downstairs; you can ask her."

Sharra guessed that was the girl she had seen serving customers while she had been speaking to Virina the innkeeper. Challin was short, plump, and very young, but an apron did not need to fit the way a tunic or skirt did. Holding her borrowed skirt in place, Sharra bent down to retrieve her dress. She picked it up and looked it over.

It was more than thirty years old, but still looked almost new, since it had spent most of that time as stone. It was not only revealing, it was, judging by what she had seen on the streets, seriously out of style. She glanced at the mattress she had been assigned. There was nowhere to hang the dress, but she could fold it up…

Or not. She didn't want to show off her body anymore. Thirty years on display was enough.

"Would you like to have this?" she asked Irith, holding it out.

Irith started. "It wouldn't fit me," she said.

"Maybe you could alter it."

"It's not long enough, and besides, I don't want to be seen in something like that. Listen, if you really don't have any money, why don't you sell it?"

Sharra opened her mouth, then closed it again. She had started to ask whether people really bought used clothing, but then she remembered seeing shops and market stalls doing exactly that. The idea of actually dealing with them had never occurred to her; she had always given her old clothes away, as selling them had seemed beneath her. Dulzan had earned enough that she did not need to bother with the few bits she might get from selling her cast-offs.

Now, though, every bit mattered.

"Do you know a good place to do that?" she asked.

"There's a shop on North Street. It's where my mother took my father's clothes after he died."

"Oh. Thank you. You've been very kind."

Irith turned up an empty palm. "We're going to be living and working together; better we get along with one another."

"Of course." Sharra glanced at the mattress that was now hers. "What happened to…Lissa, was it?"

"She moved in with her boyfriend. I expect they'll be married in a year or so – either that, or she'll move back here. She's still working some evenings."

That was a much more cheerful explanation than Sharra had expected. "Good for her!" she said.

"I suppose. *I* wouldn't want to marry Beran, but I'm not Lissa. Shouldn't you be heading back downstairs?"

"I should," Sharra agreed. She turned and headed for the stairs, holding her ugly skirt up with one hand so she wouldn't trip over the hem. She remembered wryly that Irith had made it very plain she wanted the tunic back, but had shown no such concern for the skirt.

Back in the kitchen Virina found a piece of butcher's string that could be pinned in place to secure the skirt, and Challin, during a pause in dealing with customers, unearthed an old apron that was stained with beer and stiff with spilled gravy. The thing was disgusting, but it was still technically an apron, and tying it in place helped assure that the brown skirt would stay up. That done, Challin hurried back out with two mugs of beer while Virina began instructing Sharra in the fine art of serving food and ale to sailors, longshoremen, boatmen, and the others who made up the clientele of the Crooked Mast.

CHAPTER FOURTEEN

By the end of her first shift Sharra was so exhausted she was not sure she was going to make it back up the stairs to the attic.

At least, she thought, she was young and strong again; if she had been her natural age, or even the age she had been when she first went to Poldrian's shop, she really did not think she could have survived the experience.

Or perhaps all those years standing motionless had left her feeble.

She had discovered that the promised room and board consisted of the mattress in the attic and whatever the patrons left on their plate, along with an allotted three mugs of small beer. That was, she thought, not particularly generous, but then, Virina had never claimed otherwise.

The innkeeper had been startled when Sharra asked for her pay. "Usually I pay every sixnight," Virina said.

"You said two bits per day. I worked a full day."

"And I only had one complaint about you, so…fine. Here's your money." She fished two triangular coins from the till and handed them over.

"Someone complained?" Sharra had thought she had done a good job; she had managed to not spill anything where customers could see, not even when some fool in a blue kilt had tried to trip her. Several people had been downright complimentary, though more about her looks than her serving skills.

"Emmen of Shiphaven," Virina said. "He just likes to gripe. He said you didn't smile enough and took too long with his mutton."

"It wasn't ready!"

"I know. If you'd brought it any sooner he'd have complained it was raw. You did fine, for a beginner. Go to bed. You have the morning off, but I want you ready to work by midday."

Sharra nodded, and headed up the stairs.

Virina had been right that morning in suggesting that customers might want to give her an extra coin or two. She was not entirely sure of the thinking responsible for this, since an extra bit was not about to buy much of anything; if anyone wanted something more than a smile from her, and perhaps a little extra sway of her hips, it would cost far more than one little coin. Still, she had four bits tucked into the folded waistband of her skirt, in addition to the wages in her hand; she had not mentioned that to anyone.

A bit here and a bit there could add up nicely, she thought as she climbed up to the attic.

She slept soundly. When she awoke it took her a moment to remember that she could move and open her eyes; when she did the morning light pouring through the attic window seemed impossibly bright.

She was still wearing her borrowed clothes. She took off the apron and set it aside, picked up her old dress, and made her way downstairs. To her pleased surprise she discovered that her pay included a real breakfast – two buttered flatcakes, a plump sausage, and another mug of small beer. The only drawback was that she had to clean up after herself, which meant fetching a bucket of water from the pump in the courtyard. She wondered whether leaving her apron upstairs had been a mistake, but simply took extra care to not splash anything on Irith's tunic.

When that was done she set out to North Street to see what she could get for her dress. It took some time to find the shop Irith had mentioned, and then another half-hour or so to get the shopkeeper's attention and dicker for a decent price; she was relieved to see that her bargaining skills had not been completely forgotten in her thirty years as a household ornament, and she departed with six bits in silver. She was certain the dress was worth far more, or at least that it would have been when it was the latest fashion, but now she thought she had done very well to get so much; she had argued that the buyer could market it as a precious antique, and he had apparently believed her.

She owed her mother and Dallisa a serious debt for making the dress for her; she hoped she would be able to repay them somehow.

She hoped her mother was still *alive*.

Of course, six silver bits was not a fortune, and she promptly spent one of the six bits on a good new tunic, white linen trimmed with blue silk, so she could return Irith's, and then part of another silver bit on a belt and purse. She decided to make do with the hideous skirt and grubby apron for a little longer.

As she left the shop she paused.

She had, she thought, been foolishly hasty in hurrying off, refusing Morvash's offer of help. That idea had come to her several times the previous day, but she had been too busy to do anything about it. Now she wasn't.

She stopped back at the Crooked Mast long enough to give Irith back her tunic, and then, wearing her own new one, she headed south, retracing her steps, to see if Morvash was still offering assistance.

The sun was high in the eastern sky by the time Sharra reached that strange gray house; she knew that she would need to hurry if she intended to get back to the tavern in time for her shift.

Half a dozen guardsmen were in the street in front of the house – not patrolling, but standing there, talking quietly amongst themselves. One of them stood on the front steps. Two of the big upstairs windows stood wide open, but there was no sign of anyone inside. Something appeared to have happened in the alley on one side of the house; dirt and gravel had been scattered everywhere.

Hesitantly, Sharra crossed the street and walked up to the cluster of soldiers. "Excuse me," she called.

One of the guardsmen turned to look at her, and she saw his expression change in a familiar way once he got a look at her, going from bored to both interested and wary. At least his lust was not as obvious as what she had seen when she wore the just-sold dress.

"Yes?" he asked.

"I'm looking for a wizard named Morvash of the Shadows," she said. "Is he home?"

The soldier turned to one side and called, "Lieutenant! This woman is looking for the wizard!"

Another soldier turned and looked her over as he walked closer. "Why do you want him?" he asked.

"He offered to help me with something," she said.

"You know him?"

"Well, we've met. I know he lives here."

"We don't know whether he *does* live here anymore. He and his friends left in the middle of the night, and the Wizards' Guild says that the house belongs to them now, and no one is allowed inside without the Guild's permission. Now, is there something we can help you with?"

Sharra recalled the old proverb, unasked questions go unanswered, and said, "He offered to help me get home to Ethshar of the Sands." Even as she spoke, though, she realized that was not quite true. Morvash had offered to let her stay until arrangements could be made, he had not said he would get her home.

But it did not matter. The soldier grimaced, and said, "I don't think he's in any position to do that. When he left here he was being pursued by a demon."

Sharra blinked. She knew there had been a great deal of magic involved in the preceding morning's events, but she had not realized any demons were involved. "Oh," she said.

"You weren't involved with that?"

"With a demon? No!" She shuddered, then hesitated.

She could perhaps ask someone else for help – the guards, or the Wizards' Guild – but she did not think that was likely to work very well. They had no reason to aid her, and she might wind up being questioned or imprisoned. If she wasn't back at the Crooked Mast by noon she would lose her job and the shelter of the attic.

She never should have rushed out of Morvash's house, she realized that, and when she first noticed she had no money she should have come back immediately – but she hadn't. She had been so sure she could manage without the wizard, and had not wanted to get tangled up in his affairs, particularly not his argument with the other wizard, the tall one in the dark blue robe. After what had happened with Poldrian, she hadn't wanted anything to do with *any* wizards.

And if she *had* stayed, maybe the demon would have gotten her.

"This demon," she asked. "Did it kill anyone?"

"Not that I heard, but it gave that house a good pounding."

That did not sound good. "What happened to all the people who were here yesterday morning?"

"I have no idea."

"Are they all right?"

"I just told you, I don't know – well, except for the four who were guardsmen. They all got back to camp safely."

"So you don't know what happened?"

The lieutenant sighed. "Look, all I know is that this Morvash had a spell go wrong, and a bunch of people who had been turned to stone all came back to life, but some of them were magicians and started fighting each other. The wizards all flew off somewhere, a demon showed up trying to kill some of them, and most of the rest were driven away in carriages. When it looked as if the demon was going to get through the protective spells, Morvash and his friends flew off on a magic carpet, the demon took off after him, and then people from the Wizards' Guild showed up and told us to keep everyone out and watch for anything strange. So we're here, keeping people out and watching for anything strange. Now, are you involved with any of this?"

"No," Sharra said quickly. This did not sound like anything she wanted to be any more a part of than she already was. She looked up at the wizard's house, with its turrets and dark stone walls, and decided it was time to head back to the Crooked Mast. Morvash was not here, and no one was likely to give her any help.

"Thank you," she said, turning to head back down the slope to the north.

CHAPTER FIFTEEN

By the time she had worked at the Crooked Mast for a sixnight Sharra had her own modest wardrobe, including cosmetics, and had returned all her borrowed clothes. She had learned a little bit about what had happened in her thirty years as a statue – how warlockry had vanished as abruptly as it appeared but only after a warlock named Vond had built an empire in the Small Kingdoms, how spriggans had started appearing in the city several years back and everyone had had to learn to live with the little pests, how a thief with stolen magic had declared herself Empress of Ethshar and been killed by the Wizards' Guild, and so on. The overlord of Ethshar of the Spices that she remembered, Azrad the Sedentary, had died long ago, and his son was now Azrad VII. She had missed one overlord of Ethshar of the Rocks completely – Doran IV had only ruled for a few years before dying and putting Wulran III on the throne. And back home in Ethshar of the Sands, Ederd IV had died last year at the age of eighty-four; his son was now Ederd V.

On a more personally important level she had learned that the fare to Ethshar of the Sands ranged from fifteen copper rounds to five hundred, depending on the quality of the accommodations, the speed and safety of the ship, and how much work one was willing to do while aboard. She had also learned which men (and it was only men) might give her an extra coin or two, and a few little tricks she could use to encourage them, such as smiling over her shoulder, or brushing her hip against them, or recommending a particular food or beverage – not that Sharra actually had any opinions on the fare Virina sent out, since all she got for herself, other than breakfast, was cold leftovers and the cheapest beer on the premises.

For that matter, sometimes breakfast was cold leftovers; it wasn't always as plentiful and pleasing as that first morning's.

She had already known how to fend off the men who thought her smile might mean something more was on offer; she hadn't needed that skill for a long time, but it came back readily enough.

She also learned how to chase spriggans out of the tavern. The first time she had seen one she had frozen in astonishment, but Irith had shown her how to wield a broom effectively against the little green nuisances. They did not turn up often, but Virina made it clear that when one *did* turn up, Sharra was expected to remove it immediately, before it could break or spill anything.

Not long after her arrival Sharra had met Lissa, who worked one evening and was greeted happily by some of the regular customers. Lissa was about Sharra's own height, if slightly heavier, and had a brilliant smile; in addition to the inevitable tunic, skirt, and apron, she wore a band inscribed with runes around her throat. When she and Sharra were introduced Sharra could see that the runes spelled out "Beran of Shiphaven" – presumably the name of her betrothed.

"Is that a custom here?" Sharra asked Virina, when Lissa was out of earshot. "To wear the name of one's beloved as if labeling his property?"

"I've seen it before," Virina said. "Some couples do it, some don't. If it's any comfort, Beran has a silver plate with Lissa's name on it on a chain around his throat, as well."

Sharra still found the idea unpleasant, but tried not to show it. She had been proud to claim Dulzan as her husband, but she would not have wanted his name around her throat.

Sharra had also learned that the reason her pay included lodging in the attic was that it was not safe for a pretty young woman to walk the streets of Spicetown after midnight; Lissa did not leave until Beran showed up to escort her home.

Sharra had not been foolish enough to test this herself, preferring to learn from Lissa's example and the cautionary tales Virina and Irith had told her. Challin had not contributed to these conversations; she was not inclined to talk to her new co-worker – nor to anyone else, so far as Sharra could see, at least until her brother's ship got back from the Small Kingdoms. She even kept her interactions with the customers to a minimum, and after hearing some of the unkind comments made behind her back, Sharra understood why – Challin was short and plump, with an unattractive face, and some customers were not shy about remarking on this.

Many of them treated Challin, Sharra thought, almost as if she were one of Lord Landessin's statues, rather than a person. She was an object that brought them food and drink, but still just an object to them.

Sharra had not bothered collecting her daily pay after that first night. Despite the exhaustion and sore feet, she was determined to stay on until she had saved her fare home. With twelve bits in wages, nineteen bits from customers, and two silver bits left from the sale of her dress, she felt she had made a good start. Another month or so should be enough for a berth on a small freighter.

She had thought about sending Lador a message, but she could not be sure of his address, or even that he was still alive; besides, it would have cost at least three bits to send a note with a crewman on a westbound ship, and she could not be certain the sailor would actually deliver it.

There was a time, she thought wryly, when she would have spent three bits without a second thought. It was amazing how much more aware of money she was after walking out of that wizard's house without any. Until she met Poldrian, she had never worried about money; if she didn't have enough she could get more from Dulzan, or before their marriage, from her parents.

She was thinking this over during the slow part of the afternoon when Kordis of the Old City walked in with a woman beside him. It was Irith's turn to take the next customer, and she started toward the door, but Kordis spotted Sharra and waved. Irith stopped and gave Sharra a questioning look.

"He's a friend," Sharra said, as she headed over.

"Hello, Kordis!" she said, as she approached him. "Come in!"

"Sharra!" he replied. "You're still here!"

"I am," she acknowledged. "It takes longer than this to earn passage to the Sands."

"Of course – but you haven't been kidnaped, or married, or anything."

She had guided Kordis and his companion to a table as they spoke, and now he gestured at the woman and said, "Sharra, this is my wife. Asha, this is the young woman I told you about."

"I'm pleased to meet you," Sharra said. "You are a fortunate woman; Kordis was very kind to me when we first met."

Asha stared at her, not replying. As the silence began to become uncomfortable, Sharra asked, "What can I bring you?"

"Ale," Kordis said.

Sharra nodded, and headed for the tap room. When she returned a moment later, mugs in hand, Asha asked, "Were you really kidnaped?"

"More or less," Sharra said, setting down the beers. "My nephew sold me."

"What? How could he do that?" she exclaimed.

"It's complicated," Sharra said. "I was under a spell."

"You were?" Kordis said, startled. "Is that why it was a wizard who saved you?"

"He broke the spell," Sharra confirmed.

"How terrible!" Asha said.

Sharra turned up an empty palm. "I'm fine now," she said.

"And…what sort of a spell?" Asha asked. "You're so beautiful – is this what you always looked like?"

"Asha!" Kordis gasped.

Before her petrification Sharra would have been as shocked as Kordis at such a rude question, but now, especially after listening to the inn's customers for the last few days, she was more amused than offended. She decided to admit at least part of the truth.

"No," she said. "I had a youth spell cast on me, too, and that wasn't broken." She frowned, as it occurred to her for the first time to wonder why Morvash's spell *hadn't* reversed it.

Well, wizardry didn't always make sense. Even the wizards didn't always know what it would do. And Poldrian had said that there wasn't any lingering magic, that she wouldn't *stay* young.

"So this…" Asha hesitated.

"This is what I looked like without any magic when I was eighteen or nineteen," Sharra said. "I'm older than that." She smiled wryly. "I keep telling people I'm older than I look, but nobody ever bothers to ask for an explanation."

"How *much* older?" Asha asked.

There were limits to her willingness to explain, and her thirty years as a statue made any simple answer misleading. "Older," Sharra said.

"You're beautiful."

"I know. And I used to think that was really important, but I learned better." She gestured at Kordis. "You have a good man who loves you, so I'd guess that in addition to being pretty, you have more important qualities than mere beauty."

Asha's mouth opened, but she did not say a word; instead she blushed.

Kordis smiled fondly at Asha, and then looked back at Sharra. "You did say you were older, but I didn't think you meant *magic*," he said.

"I didn't think it was a good idea to mention it," she said. "Some people have very strange ideas about magic." She paused, then added, "As if magic isn't strange enough without making things up!"

Asha smiled uncertainly.

"Did you come here just to see me, or can I get you anything else?"

"I wanted to see you," Asha said. "Kordis had been worried about you, and I wanted to see who it was that had him so concerned."

"You were worried?" Sharra asked him, startled.

"A little. You were all alone in a strange city, with no money, and wearing that dress..."

Sharra smiled. "I was able to sell that silly thing for good money once I had something else to wear. Honestly, Kordis, I'm fine. I told you I can take care of myself."

"You did, but...well, I thought you *were* as young as you look, even though you told me you weren't."

"I'm getting used to that." She glanced in the direction of the kitchen door and saw Virina eyeing her. "I need to attend to my work, but it was wonderful to see you, Kordis, and a pleasure to meet you, Asha."

She turned away and hurried over to Virina to see what she should do next.

Virina wanted her to talk Kordis and Asha into buying more, and Sharra did make an attempt, but the best she could do was another round of ale; after that the couple settled their bill and left, leaving four bits more for Sharra.

As she tucked the coins away, it occurred to Sharra that she was collecting money she had not really earned, simply because she was beautiful. She knew that Irith and Challin, who worked just as hard as she did, never got more than a bit or two – if that.

It wasn't fair. She was no longer *trying* to take advantage of her appearance as she had when she really was young, but she was still being rewarded for it.

When she was young and trying to coax favors from everyone around her, up to and including convincing Dulzan to marry her, she had thought it was only right that she, the prettiest, should receive these extras. Then she had thought that she deserved the best because she was married to a great craftsman, and she had still taken pride in her appearance, as well.

But she had made Dulzan miserable, and she had estranged her sisters, and once she was no longer young and marriageable no one had really cared what she looked like. Oh, from time to time she had overheard a few people congratulating Dulzan on marrying such a beauty, right up until he left her, but in the end no one had liked her any better because of her appearance, not really.

When she was a statue she had heard several people, mostly men, comment on her beauty, but nothing had ever come of it. None of them had ever expressed any interest in her beyond a single remark; none had ever *repeated* their praise, or expanded upon it, or inquired after the sculptor responsible for her appearance – at least, not until Morvash had begun testing to see which statues were really alive. All her beauty had meant was that people, especially men, enjoyed looking at her, and that was all it meant now that she was alive again. It didn't mean they *liked* her; it just meant they liked *looking* at her, and at least part of that was not esthetics, but lust. Even if she never gave them the slightest encouragement, she could tell that some of them were imagining what it would be like to take her to bed – and not just the ones who actually tried to talk her into it, either. Even Kordis, who was clearly devoted to his wife, had left her extra coins.

Except for Kordis, none of her customers knew a thing about her beyond her appearance, but they smiled at her and gave her money, while poor Challin was completely ignored.

That was not something to be proud of.

On the other hand, it was definitely helpful in saving up her fare back to Ethshar of the Sands. She *was* beautiful, and it wouldn't help Irith or Challin if she *didn't* accept the extra money it brought in.

She could have split the money with the other women, and she felt slightly guilty that she was not doing so, but she needed the money to get *home*. So she kept it, even though it wasn't fair.

Life, she thought, was not fair.

When she had said that thirty or forty years ago, before Dulzan left her, she had meant it wasn't fair that she couldn't have everything she wanted; now she meant the opposite, that she was benefitting from something that wasn't her doing, but just luck.

Or perhaps it *was* her doing, in that she had bought a youth spell, but all that had done was given her back what time had taken away. It was still something she had been lucky enough to be born with.

She remembered those fancy parties at the overlord's palace when she had swept around the room displaying her fine clothes, sure that everyone there admired and envied her, sure that Dulzan loved and admired her...

She had been an idiot. She had refused to see that Dulzan hadn't loved her in years. And all the others – she remembered how so many of them had hurried away after just a few words, and she had always looked on it as an opportunity to move on to the next person she wanted to impress, but now she realized most of them had not wanted to talk to her. She had been arrogant and self-centered and *boring*, unwilling to talk about anything but herself and her ambitions.

Here at the inn her only ambition was to save up the money to get home, and she had not cared about impressing Irith or Challin or Virina. She didn't think any of them really *liked* her, not really – she had not been willing to share much about herself because she didn't intend to stay and she didn't want to explain how she had spent the last thirty years – but they didn't seem to mind her company. She and Irith had traded some stories about customers, and shared a laugh or two, and Sharra realized she could not remember a time when she had laughed with a friend, rather than laughing alone at some poor unfortunate, for at least ten years *before* Poldrian had petrified her. She remembered Dulzan asking her when she had last laughed, and she had said it was when Thed the Younger fell off the pier, but she had not recalled until later that she had been the *only* one who laughed at poor Thed. No one else had found the boy's predicament funny.

She had, because she hadn't cared whether or not he drowned.

She had spent thirty years listening to other people without their knowledge, unable to speak, and with far too much time to think, and she had discovered that listening to people like her old self was unpleasant.

She had a chance to start over, to be someone new, someone better, and she knew she shouldn't waste it. Perhaps she could, in time, be a real friend to Irith and Challin.

But she still wanted to get home to her family, and befriending anyone on the way was less important than getting home as quickly as she could.

CHAPTER SIXTEEN

She knew it wasn't enough for a luxurious ride, but by the middle of Newfrost Sharra thought she finally had enough money saved to get back to Ethshar of the Sands, and she really wanted to get to sea before the winter storms really set in. Since her mornings were her own, she had begun spending them wandering from ship to ship, inquiring about what it would cost to get home.

Most of the ships were headed the wrong direction, across the Gulf of the East to the Small Kingdoms, but some were bound westward. It took her a little while to realize that anything bound for either side of Tintallion, or Shan on the Sea, or Ethshar of the Rocks would put in at Ethshar of the Sands along the way, forcing her to backtrack – there were three places she had asked only, "Where are you bound?" and not inquired about intermediate stops, even though they were going in the right direction.

She also heard a few rumors; apparently Morvash had returned from wherever he had gone, and was back in the house on Old East Avenue. She considered going to see him, but decided not to bother. Finding passage home was more important.

And on the 27th of Newfrost she found a ship's captain whose opening bid was not hopelessly out of her range.

It took almost an hour of dickering to finally agree on a fare that would leave a few coins in her pocket; the captain had been in no hurry to reach an agreement, since the ship was being loaded and would not depart until the evening tide, but Sharra had to run to get back to the Crooked Mast before her shift.

She explained the situation to Virina – she would need to leave early, and would not be coming back. Virina was not, to say the least, happy about this news.

"You could have given me more warning," she grumbled.

"I told you all along I was looking for a ship that could take me home!" Sharra protested.

"I know, but I thought you'd give me at least a full day's notice!"

"I would have if I could, but the ship sails with this afternoon's tide, an hour before sunset."

"And what if I insist you finish your shift?"

"Unless you put a geas on me, I'll leave anyway."

Virina frowned. "Fine." She waved a dismissal. "Go, then. I hope your voyage is a safe one, but don't expect a full day's wages."

"Thank you," Sharra replied, startled. She had not expected to be paid again at all, and was only working these last few hours as a favor to Virina – and of course, she wouldn't object if a few customers slipped her an extra coin or two. She nodded – almost a bow, rally – then hurried to get her apron.

Around mid-afternoon, during a lull in business, she collected her meager belongings from the attic, wrapped them into a manageable bundle, and heaved them up on her shoulder. When she had them arranged comfortably she made her way carefully down the stairs.

At the bottom she found Challin staring at her.

"You're really going?" Challin asked.

Sharra nodded.

"I'll miss you," Challin said.

Sharra barely caught herself in time to not say, "You will?" She and Challin had hardly ever spoken to one another. She didn't know what to say instead, and just smiled.

"Safe travels," Challin said.

"Thank you."

The ship was called the *Sharpened Blade*, and it belonged to three brothers – Bragen the Strong, Kargan the Armorer, and Gror the Merchant. She recognized the names, of course, and found the coincidence amusing – it seemed she would be getting some help from Morvash's family after all.

The ship was bound for Tintallion of the Coast with a cargo of weapons, but would put in for supplies at Ethshar of the Sands and Ethshar of the Rocks. Sharra would be sleeping in a curtained-off alcove, not a cabin of her own – she had known that when she agreed to the price. The voyage to Ethshar of the Sands was expected to last five or six days, perhaps a little more; they could not afford a magician who could ensure favorable winds, but there was no reason to think the weather would be particularly uncooperative.

The sailors were standing ready to cast off when Sharra came running up; the instant she was across the gangplank and aboard, the captain took her arm and pulled her out of the way so that the crew could get the ship underway.

"Stay out of the way until we're out at sea," he told her. "You can go below, if you like."

"I want to watch!" Sharra protested.

"Fine. Just stay out of the way."

She did her best to oblige, standing well clear as the lines were hauled in and the sails hoisted, but crewmen seemed to be everywhere on the deck and more than once she had to hurry out of someone's path.

At last, though, the sails were in place and the ship was clear of the port, making her way northeast. Sharra watched the city and its walls dwindle behind them, and finally vanish as the ship swung to starboard and headed east, along the sandy shores of the Peninsula. The sun was setting now, its red glow lighting the yellow-painted sails a rich golden orange. The sea air was fresh and sharp, utterly unlike the smoky, sweaty odor of the Crooked Mast's dining room.

One of the ship's crew came and stood beside Sharra as she watched the distant land slide by.

"Unless the moons are very bright or the captain has hired some new magic, we'll probably anchor before full dark," he said. "Rounding the headland from Azrad's Bay into the main body of the Gulf isn't safe by night."

Sharra glanced at him but said nothing.

"I hear you're bound for Ethshar of the Sands."

She nodded, still not speaking.

"Any particular reason? Or are you just looking for adventure?"

"I'm going home," she said, reluctantly breaking her silence.

"Are you? Why were you in Ethshar of the Spices, then?"

"I was kidnaped. By someone who thought I would make a nice ornament for his mansion."

The crewman blinked.

"He's dead now," she added. "A wizard rescued me."

"Oh," the crewman said. His voice had lost much of its enthusiasm. He had clearly thought that a pretty young woman traveling alone might be an easy target for him, but Sharra guessed he was now experiencing doubts. Getting involved with kidnapers and wizards might have unwanted complications, and a woman who had been through such an experience was probably not going to be as gullible as he had hoped.

"Kelder!" someone called. "Stop bothering the passenger and go fetch the lead; the captain's called for sounding."

"Coming!" Kelder called back. Then he turned to Sharra again and said, "It's been a pleasure meeting you. I hope we'll have a chance to speak again."

She did not reply beyond a slight nod.

The next time she heard Kelder's voice was ten minutes later, as he bellowed from somewhere forward, "No bottom with this line!"

A man whose blue cap bore a green and white cockade stopped by her and said, "I'm Horl, second mate. I hope Kelder wasn't bothering you earlier."

"Not really. He said we might be anchoring for the night?"

Horl shook his head. "That's why he's in the chains right now, testing the depth – so we won't need to anchor. If it starts to shoal... I mean, if the water gets dangerously shallow, the captain might reconsider, but he's hoping to sail right through the night."

"Nine fathoms!" Kelder called.

"Let me know if any of the crew bother you, or if there's anything I can do for you." Then without waiting for a reply he touched his cheek and walked away.

No one else spoke to her for the rest of the evening. As the sunlight faded in the west a dozen lanterns were lit, all around the deck, and Kelder kept calling out the depth. The line apparently didn't reach more than ten fathoms, and by the time Sharra grew weary and retired to her bunk the depth had varied from three to ten fathoms. At three fathoms the captain had ordered a turn to port, presumably to reach deeper water.

Kelder's reports continued, and she could hear them from her alcove, but they were muffled and distant; they did keep her awake for a few minutes, but in time they became oddly comforting and she dozed off.

They had apparently reached deep water while she slept; when she awoke no one was calling out depths, though there were occasional shouted orders and running feet. She climbed out of her berth and found that the sun was brightening the sky but had not yet cleared the horizon – and assuming the sun still rose in the east, they were heading due south. Land was visible in the distance on both sides, but much closer on the western side.

By that afternoon they had finally turned west, and the only land in sight was to the north. Even that vanished into the mist soon enough.

None of the crewmen spoke to her uninvited; apparently word had gotten around that she was not quite the young innocent she looked, or perhaps someone had warned them to leave her alone. There were a few women in the crew, though, mostly older looking – though she realized, with some amusement, that she was probably decades older than any of them, and most likely the oldest person on the ship. Two of them, Liliz the Sailmaker and Derrin the Witch, took time to chat with her.

Derrin, of course, was the ship's magician, and while her specialties were weather prediction and sensing approaching threats, she was called on to act as the ship's healer, mediator, and mender as well. She was initially friendly, approaching Sharra in a motherly fashion, but then she seemed to sense something was off about their passenger, and she retreated in apparent confusion.

Despite her cognomen, Liliz did far more than make sails; she also served as the ship's quartermaster, making and repairing the sailors' uniforms. She was delighted when she learned that Sharra had once been apprenticed to a weaver; it gave her a chance to discuss sewing and tailoring, subjects in which no one else aboard was remotely interested. Sharra was not particularly interested herself, but she wanted to be polite, and after so long in the crowded, noisy tavern she was not entirely comfortable being left to herself on the ship's deck, and welcomed the conversation, even if she had little to contribute.

"I'll tell you," Liliz said, as she and Sharra leaned on the starboard rail, "I'm glad that sailors wear kilts! You could offer me eternal youth for them, and I still couldn't sew a decent pair of breeches."

Sharra had heard the expression before, but something about it caught her attention. "It costs far more than a pair of breeches for an eternal youth spell," she replied.

"Oh, I'm sure it does," Liliz agreed. "It's just a saying."

"A youth spell can cost seventy-five rounds of gold, and not even be an eternal one." She was once again thinking how much money she had wasted.

For a moment Liliz didn't respond, but then she said, "Seventy-five rounds? That's oddly specific."

"It's not odd."

"You've bought one?"

Sharra nodded. "It was a mistake," she said.

"Do you want to talk about it?"

To her own surprise, Sharra realized that she did. "I was married for twenty years," she said. "When my husband told me he was leaving, I bought the spell to lure him back. It didn't work."

"Twenty years."

Sharra nodded. "I knew he'd married me for my looks, so I thought if I looked the way I did when we were married he would stay. He didn't."

"He grew up, I suppose," Liliz said.

"And I hadn't," Sharra agreed.

"You hadn't?"

"No. If I had, I'd have known it wouldn't work. I really, truly hadn't. But I'm working on it now."

"Twenty years – so you're…"

"Older than I look. It's complicated." She sighed. "Let's just say I can remember the Night of Madness." That had been about thirty-seven years ago, when she had still been married – happily, she had thought – to Dulzan.

"Well, so do I, for that…" Then Liliz took another look at Sharra. "Oh," she said. "So you bought a youth spell. I take it that it worked?"

Sharra nodded.

"Was that in Ethshar of the Sands?"

"Yes. From a wizard named Poldrian of Morningside. And we had a disagreement about the bill."

"Is it safe for you to be going back, then?"

That, Sharra realized, was a question she had not dared ask herself. How *was* Poldrian going to react if she turned up alive? Morvash had said he wouldn't bother her, but could she be sure of that? Would he still want the money?

"I'm told he considers it over and done with," she said.

"I hope that's true."

"*I* hope someone still remembers me," Sharra said. Morvash had said Poldrian was still alive, but who else was? Who wasn't? She knew her father was gone, but what about her mother? She would be in her nineties – her *late* nineties.

She was probably gone.

Dallisa and Nerra would be old women. Dulzan…what had become of Dulzan?

"Why wouldn't they remember you?" Liliz asked. "A youth spell wouldn't change that."

"It's complicated," Sharra replied. She was not quite sure why she was so reluctant to tell anyone she had spent thirty years as a statue, even someone she would probably never see again after they reached Ethshar of the Sands, but it felt too intimate, somehow.

Liliz turned up an empty palm, and the conversation ended.

That evening Derrin found Sharra on the afterdeck, in the shadow of the sails, looking out at the ship's wake. "Liliz tells me you had a youth spell put on you," she said.

Sharra glanced at the witch, then continued looking over the rail at the sea. "I did," she said.

"I knew *something* felt strange about you."

Sharra did not reply.

"Will you always look like this?"

Sharra shook her head. "No, no. I'm aging normally, or at least I'm supposed to be. I just got a reset."

"How old are you really?"

"It's complicated."

"Well, how complicated…" She sensed, a little belatedly, that Sharra did not want to explain, and did not finish her question. Instead she said, "You're going home?"

"Yes."

"Were you away long?"

"It's complicated," Sharra repeated.

"How can…" Derrin cut herself off again. "Was there more magic involved?"

"Yes."

After a pause, Derrin asked, "Do you have family waiting for you? Or friends?"

"I don't know," Sharra said. "I *wish* I knew. But I don't. I hope I do." She looked out at the sea. "I really, really hope so."

CHAPTER SEVENTEEN

It was perhaps an hour before midday on the second of Snowfall when the *Sharpened Blade* tied up at Third Pier, midway between the Outer and Inner Towers of Seagate Harbor. Sharra had splurged on a few items beyond the basic ship's fare, mostly sweets, and had to devote a few minutes to settling the bill for incidentals before the purser would allow her off the ship; after doing so she found her savings reduced to a mere three bits. She hoped she would be able to find *someone* she knew who could give her a place to stay, or she might be spending the night in the Wall Street Field.

By the time Sharra had satisfied the purser and packed up her belongings the sun was almost as high in the sky as it was going to get, and loading was well underway – nothing was being *unloaded* in Ethshar of the Sands except herself. She had to wait for a break in the stream of provisions being brought on board for the next leg of the journey before she was able to make her way down the gangplank; the captain wanted to catch the next high tide, which meant rushing to get everything stowed.

At last, though, she was off the ship and once again on solid ground – or at least, on the North Causeway. Eager to get back to familiar territory, or at least territory she *hoped* would be familiar, she hurried across the southern tip of the West Beaches, past the Inner Towers, into Seagate. As she did, she noticed that Ethshar of the Sands was infested with spriggans, just like Ethshar of the Spices; three of them were being chased around the beach by local children.

Once she was in the city itself it was still about two miles to her mother's shop on Weaver Street, so she bought a slab of fried onion bread from a tent on Seagate Street to eat as she walked. That cost her a copper bit, one-third of her entire fortune, but it tasted better than any of the fare she had eaten on the ship, or back at the Crooked Mast – in fact, she could not remember ever eating anything better. She was not entirely sure whether it was really that good, or whether she just enjoyed getting a familiar treat she had not eaten in more than thirty years.

Straight West Street took her through Seagate to the Merchants' Quarter, where she wound her way south through a tangle of nameless byways to Copper Street and turned east again. She had finished the onion bread by then.

This took her into the part of the city she had lived in, but she did not yet recognize anything. Copper Street looked familiar, but in an unspecific way – the shops and buildings were all the sort of thing she would expect to find there, but she did not see a single name she recognized on any of the signboards.

Finally she came to the shrine at the corner of Copper and Glassblower Street, which was something she remembered, though the statue of Piskor was noticeably more weathered than it had been when she last saw it.

Thirty years would explain that. *She* had not weathered visibly despite being a statue, but she had been indoors, and perhaps chalcedony was harder than whatever this figure was made of. What would have happened if she *had* been damaged while petrified?

She would probably never know, and she was very glad of that.

A block later she turned right on South Dock Street, where some taverns still bore the names she knew; she was not sure about any of the shops.

Five blocks later she turned east on Spinner Street and followed it across South Street, moving from the Merchants' Quarter into Crafton. Then she just had to go one more block down the slope to the south, and she was on Weaver Street.

It was still unmistakably Weaver Street, where she had grown up; she could hear the familiar clatter of looms and smell the dyes and fabrics, and the windows displayed bright fabrics of every kind.

Once or twice he thought she saw a passerby start at the sight of her – could it be they actually recognized her after so long?

And then she saw the sign ahead, but it no longer said KIRSHA THE WEAVER, FINE FABRICS – now it read simply LADOR THE WEAVER, and the second line had been painted over with a red-and-gold curlicue. The paint was flaking; apparently Lador had not bothered to touch it up, and had not had any preservative magic put on it.

But it was still the same shop, and this Lador was undoubtedly her nephew. She took a deep breath, strode forward, opened the door and stepped inside.

The bell jingled, and the man behind the counter looked up. His jaw dropped, and he stared at her.

She kept her own face under better control, but her eyes did widen. "Lador?" she said, a little uncertainly.

He had gained twenty or thirty pounds, none of it muscle; his head was bald and shining, but as if to compensate his beard had grown out and reached to his chest. Still, she was fairly certain it really was her nephew.

He looked shabby. So did the shop, for that matter, and it was hardly good advertising for a weaver to wear so faded a tunic. Her mother would never have allowed it.

"Aunt *Sharra*?" he exclaimed. "Aunt Sharra? You're back?"

"Not because of anything *you* did," she retorted.

"It's really you? After all this time?" He was staring at her as if she were an especially spectacular illusion in an arena magic show.

"Yes, it's me," she said, annoyed by his reaction.

"You haven't aged a day!"

"I've aged a month and a half," she said. "It took me some time to get back here."

"You look as young as ever, and even more beautiful than I remember!"

"*You* don't." All the politeness and flirtatiousness she had carefully developed while working at the Crooked Mast had vanished in an instant upon seeing Lador and her parents' shop both so dreadfully changed.

"Well, after all, it's been thirty years!"

"And whose fault is that?" She put her hands on her hips and glared at him. "Why didn't you ever rescue me?"

"I...I could never come up with the money, Aunt. I *tried*, I swear I did, but..." He waved a hand, taking in their surroundings. "The fact is, Aunt, I'm not a very good weaver, and I'm not very good with money. I don't know how Grandmother did it. I could never save enough to pay your debt."

"How much *did* you save? How close were you?"

"I...well, I...how did you get turned back, Aunt? Did someone else pay the wizard – Polidan, was it?"

"Poldrian. You don't even remember his *name*? How were you going to pay him if you didn't know his name?"

"I've been busy! It's been thirty years!"

"Which I would have *thought* was long enough to raise that sixteen rounds of gold, especially since you got six and a half by selling me to Lord Landessin. You only needed another nine and a half. So how close were you?"

Lador looked down. "I...wasn't very close."

"How much?"

"I had twelve rounds."

"Twelve out of sixteen?" She frowned. "That's not as bad as I feared..."

"No, Aunt Sharra," he interrupted. "Twelve out of twenty-five."

She stared silently at him for several seconds, her mouth tight, before eventually saying, slowly, "You just have twelve rounds of gold?"

"Yes." He nodded miserably.

"You had more than *fifteen* when Lord Landessin's men carried me off to Ethshar of the Spices! The nine I had, and the money he paid for his confounded statue!"

"I told you I wasn't good with money."

"It wasn't your money!"

"I know."

She glared at him for a moment, then looked up at the ceiling – which had cobwebs on it, she noticed.

It wasn't so very bad, she told herself. Twelve rounds of gold was still a lot of money. She could be comfortable for quite some time with that much. She certainly wouldn't need to wait on tables. She lowered her gaze again. "Where is it?" she asked.

"My mother has it," Lador said.

"Your mother? Dallisa has it? Why?"

"So I won't lose any more of it," Lador admitted, cringing.

Sharra paused for a moment, considering. That was actually probably a good thing. Dallisa was not her favorite person in the World, but she was probably more trustworthy than her son.

Probably.

"Whose idea was that?"

"Mine."

At least Lador had recognized his own susceptibility to the temptation that money had posed. Maybe he wasn't completely hopeless.

"Where is she?"

"My parents still live on Spinner Street," he said, in a tone of mild surprise. "They sold the shop, though."

"And the money is there?"

"I don't know. I thought it would be better if I didn't."

It seemed Lador was wise enough to recognize his own failings. That was something *she* hadn't managed until she had spent some time as a statue, unwillingly eavesdropping on her family.

For an awkward moment neither of them spoke; then Lador repeated, "How did you get turned back?"

"A wizard named Morvash took pity on me," Sharra said. "Not just me; he had an entire collection of people who had been turned to stone, and he transformed all of us back to men and women."

"Oh," Lador said.

Sharra turned to look out the shop window. The sun was still bright, and she saw no sign of sunset colors; it probably wasn't any later than mid-afternoon. Dallisa might be out at the market, or working on something important; finding her could wait a little. "Lador," she said, "is my mother still alive?"

"Grandmother? Oh, yes. She's…well, she's ninety-seven. She's not very…she gets confused easily. She still talks to Grandfather sometimes, and he's been gone for more than twenty years. She lives with Aunt Nerra and Uncle Kovan."

"Then they're all right?"

"Oh, Aunt Nerra and Uncle Kovan are fine. They still have the shop on Carder Street, with two assistants and occasional apprentices. Their daughter Thetheran is married now, with four kids of her own; they have a farm north of the city, where her husband Zorl is from, but we see them every year on Festival. Shesha went off with a sailor from the Small Kingdoms and we haven't heard from her in ages. Gorbal is living with his boyfriend in Beachgate – they work for the Arena. Lorza drowned when his boat was caught in a storm. Amari married a wizard named Gorazin the Magnificent, but left him after he accidentally turned her into a cat and took a month to change her back because he was too busy with paying customers; she and her daughter have a place in Southshore and do odd jobs, and Gorazin makes sure they don't starve."

Sharra did not think she could have named all of Nerra's children, and definitely didn't think she would be able to keep all that straight. "What about *your* sister?" she asked. "Mama had wanted Arris to take over here, but that obviously didn't happen."

"Arris? When she made master she left that fool Tresh that she had married when she was a journeyman, and married a captain in the city guard instead. I like him. His name is Bolnar; they and their three sons live up in Grandgate, near the barracks, and her shop there has a contract to provide the cloth for the guard's blankets and winter cloaks."

"That must keep her busy."

"She gives me any work her shop can't handle. Sometimes it's the only thing that keeps me in business."

Sharra frowned. "How did *you* wind up with this shop? Arris is older, and your mother or Nerra would have a claim."

"No one else wanted to work for Grandmother; they all wanted their own places. I started out as Grandmother's assistant, and when she couldn't work any more I just stayed on. I waited a year after she left before I repainted the sign, but that 'fine fabrics' wasn't what I was doing, so as long as I was changing that, I changed the name."

"So it's just you?"

"It's just me."

"You aren't married?"

"I was for awhile, but Zinni left me years ago, after our two little girls died of fever. I don't know where she is now."

Sharra didn't remember anyone named Zinni, but losing two children must have been horrible. "I'm sorry," she said. She wished she had met those grandnieces. She wished she had even known they *existed*.

"It's all right," Lador said. "It was long ago."

"And..." She hesitated, but decided she had to ask. "Dulzan?"

Lador did not appear surprised. "He still has his shop on Carpenter Street, I think, but he doesn't take many commissions anymore, or maybe he doesn't take *any*, and he hasn't done anything *but* commissions since you...since you left. I haven't talked to him in years."

He made no mention of any family. Sharra remembered how she had assumed Dulzan had left her for another woman; now she hoped he had found one, at least for a little while. She didn't want him to have lived all those years alone.

She wasn't mad at him for leaving her; she never had been, not really, and any lingering anger had faded long ago. She had deserved it.

Of course, if he wanted her back…but she didn't think he would.

"Was there anything else, Aunt?" Lador asked.

"I don't have any money left, or anywhere to stay tonight," Sharra said. "I think it's time to pay your mother a visit and get my money back. Would you take me there?"

"I have to stay here," Lador said. "There's no one else to mind the shop. But you must know where the house is."

Sharra was ashamed to admit to herself that she did not. She did not remember ever visiting Dallisa and her husband. She had to think for a moment even to remember his name – Shaldar the Tailor. "It's been a long time," she said. "Remind me."

CHAPTER EIGHTEEN

The directions were simple enough, and five minutes after she left the shop on Weaver Street Sharra was on Spinner Street, knocking on her sister's door.

"I'm coming!" a familiar voice called – but not quite the voice Sharra remembered; this voice was pitched a little higher and not entirely steady. Then the door opened, and Sharra found herself face to face with an old woman she did not recognize at first.

Before she could say anything, though, the old woman exclaimed, "Sharra! You're back!" Then her eyes narrowed. "But how? Lador said he gave me all of the money."

This woman was indeed Dallisa. The thirty years since Sharra last saw her had not been particularly kind; her hair was snow white and thinning, she had developed a good many wrinkles, and she was hunched a little – she had always been slightly shorter than Sharra, but now the difference was much more noticeable, no longer slight.

But beneath the wrinkles, it was still the same face. And that immediate suspicion and the instant focus on money – that was Dallisa.

"A wizard named Morvash did it," Sharra said. "He made a project out of rescuing people who had been turned to stone. For free."

"It's really you?"

"It's really me."

"Oh! Well, come in, come in, and tell me about it." She stepped aside, and gestured Sharra into a cozy parlor. "Can I get you something to drink?"

"That would be very welcome."

"Tea?"

"Fine."

Dallisa vanished into the kitchen, and after standing awkwardly in the center of the room for a moment, Sharra settled into the nearest chair. She had noticed the one big, comfortable-looking armchair that looked as if it saw the most use, but she decided against taking it; she guessed that was Dallisa's or Shaldar's favorite, and she was trying to break her old selfish habits.

She was fairly certain she had never been in this room before. If she had ever visited this house before – and she wasn't sure of that – she had spent her time in the kitchen. All her memories of Dallisa as an adult were in kitchens, or in a shop, sewing.

She hadn't been invited into the kitchen, though. She realized she was being treated as a guest now, not as family.

But she *was* family! She was still Dallisa's younger sister.

Dallisa reappeared with a tray holding two mugs and a teapot; she set it on a table, then settled into the big armchair. For a moment, neither woman spoke. Dallisa poured tea into both mugs, then handed one to Sharra; she accepted it, but did not drink, as it was still too hot. Instead she sat there, mug in hand, looking at her sister.

Dallisa was seven years older than she was, which meant... Sharra struggled for a moment with the arithmetic, unable to believe that she was sixty-nine and Dallisa was seventy-six. She had not worked out the numbers before.

Dallisa blew on her own tea, then looked at Sharra. "So what happened?" she asked.

Sharra frowned, struggling with the question. "Where should I start?" she said.

"What *happened*?"

"I...don't know where you want me to start."

Dallisa looked annoyed, then said, "You and Dulzan had a place in Brightside, on Straight South Street, and then he left you, and... did you really sell the house to buy a youth spell?"

"Yes," Sharra admitted. "I did. It was stupid. I thought if I looked like this again he'd come back."

"But he didn't."

"No, he didn't. He knew better, even if I didn't. I was still the same person he knew he didn't want."

"But you bought the spell, and it worked – are you *always* going to look like that? You'll be young forever?"

"No, no." Sharra waved her free hand, and shook her head. "No, I'm going to age just like anyone else, or at least that's what Poldrian told me. He just made me about twenty years younger."

"Poldrian is the wizard who enchanted you?"

"That's right. Poldrian of Morningside."

"And you couldn't pay him. I made you those dresses so you could try to coax money out of someone to pay him, and I talked Milsin and her troupe into dancing to give you good luck. But that was more than thirty years ago; why do you *still* look as if you just turned nineteen?"

Sharra was too shocked to reply immediately. Dallisa stared at her silently, and at last she said, "*Statues* don't age!"

"Well, I knew you were turned to stone, I saw that, but…how long did that last? I don't understand how that worked. You aren't stone *now*; did it wear off? Or did the dancers' magic cure you?"

Sharra blinked. "No, Morvash turned me back. I told you that."

"Yes, you did say that. And when did that happen?"

"Just a few sixnights ago, on the 26th of Leafcolor. Then I worked as a barmaid until I had enough money to buy passage home, and here I am."

"Leafcolor? Leafcolor of *this year*?"

"Yes."

"I thought it must have happened long ago!"

"No."

"So you spent *thirty years* as a statue?"

"Yes."

"That must have been horrible!"

"It was. I couldn't move or talk, and I was blind, but I could still hear."

"You were…you weren't asleep?"

"For thirty years? No."

"And you're still…did you stay young that whole time? Or did this Morvash make you young again when he turned you back?"

"No, I stayed like this. Stone doesn't age. When he turned me back I looked just the same as when Poldrian petrified me."

"Even after thirty years?"

"Yes." Sharra was puzzled; Dallisa had always been quick-witted, and had never needed detailed explanations. Why was she having such difficulty understanding the situation?

Then Sharra looked at her sister's face again and remembered. Dallisa was seventy-six. She was *old* – and some old people had trouble keeping their thoughts straight. She sipped tea as she tried to think what she should say next.

"Why did Morvash turn you back? Where did you get the money? I didn't give it to you; did Shaldar?"

"No, Dallisa. There wasn't any money involved. Morvash just thought it wasn't fair to leave me a statue forever."

"That was kind of him."

"Yes, it was," Sharra agreed, realizing she had never thanked Morvash.

"You said that happened in Leafcolor, over a month ago; why didn't you come to see me sooner? Why hadn't I heard you were alive again?"

"Well, I was in Ethshar of the Spices, and it took some time to earn my fare back."

"Why were you in Ethshar of the *Spices*?"

"Lador didn't tell you?"

"Tell me what?"

"He sold me," Sharra said, and a twinge of anger stirred within her. "He *sold* me, to a man who collected statues. He said he did it to get more of the money he needed to pay to have me turned back. And the buyer, Lord Landessin, took me back to his mansion in Ethshar of the Spices."

"I knew Lador was collecting money to get you turned back, of course, but…he *sold* you? We all thought he just put you away somewhere out of sight. Mama hated seeing you like that."

"He sold me," Sharra said. "I thought it meant he would have enough to pay Poldrian soon, but that…well, I don't know when it was, but it must have been at least twenty years ago, and he never did pay."

"Lador was never good with money. He gave the money to me and Shaldar to keep until someone thought of a way to raise the rest. And no one ever did."

"Yes, he told me. That's why I came here. I'd like it back."

"Like what back?"

"My money."

"Oh, but…it's not yours, it's Lador's."

Sharra stared at her sister. "No, it isn't; it's *mine*. Lador was just holding it for me."

"It's Lador's."

"It's *mine*. I hid it in the shop, and Lador found it. And then he sold me for six and a half gold rounds, which he had no right to do – that's *definitely* mine."

"Sounds to me as if *that* part belongs to this Lord whatever who bought the statue," Dallisa argued. "He didn't get to keep what he paid it for."

"Lord Landessin is dead!"

"And the rest belongs to that wizard, Poldrian."

"That's ridiculous!"

Dallisa turned up an empty palm. "Maybe it belongs to this Morvash, then, since he was the one who turned you back, but I don't see any way it's *yours*."

"I was the one who hid it in the shop!"

"Not all of it."

"No, not all of it, but nine rounds."

"I think we need to have a magistrate settle this."

Sharra stared silently at her sister for a moment, at the dry white hair and the wrinkled face and the defiant, self-satisfied smile she was trying to hide.

Dallisa was *enjoying* this, Sharra realized. She was getting back at her selfish, trouble-making little sister who somehow looked fifty years younger than her actual age, and was not going to ever again be her proper age. Dallisa had probably never been as confused as she had pretended to be.

And the chance to keep all that money…did Dallisa still *have* the money, or had she spent it?

No, she probably still had it, and quite possibly a lot more. She wasn't a spendthrift like her son. She might have the entire twenty-five rounds Poldrian had demanded, but had not wanted to spend it on Sharra.

"All right," Sharra said. "I'll ask Lador to get it back, and we can see what the magistrate says." She stood up. "It's been good seeing you, Dallisa."

Startled, Dallisa said, "You're going?"

"I am. I'm sorry I bothered you. Thank you for making those dresses; the one I was wearing as a statue turned out to be very helpful when I sold it. Feel free to subtract six bits of silver from the money you're holding. Give Shaldar my best wishes." Then she turned and headed for the door.

Behind her, Dallisa called, "Wait, Sharra!"

"Goodbye. I'll let myself out."

And then she was back on Embroidery Street, closing the door behind her, and a gust of wind reminded her that she had no coat and winter was coming.

She hesitated, unsure where to go. She obviously couldn't afford a place of her own, with Dallisa refusing to return the money, but there had to be somewhere. Lador had told her that Nerra and Kovan still had the shop on Carder Street, and were prospering, with apprentices and assistants; surely they would take her in for a night or two if she asked.

And that was where Mama was staying.

She shivered. She did not think she was ready to see what thirty years had done to her mother. Seeing first Lador and then Dallisa had been enough of a shock for one day – and wouldn't her reappearance be at least as great a shock for Mama? If she was really as old and fragile as Lador had said, it might kill her.

She would want someone to warn her mother, break the news to her carefully; she didn't dare just walk in.

Besides, what if Nerra was as unwelcoming as Dallisa? They had never really been very close, even as children – *no one* had been very close to her, except Mama and Dulzan, and she had badly misjudged her relationship with Dulzan.

There were the other nieces and nephews, of course, but she was not sure where to find them. She could go back to Lador, but that idea was not appealing at all.

She wished she had a coat. At least she wasn't wearing that dress she had been petrified in, the one she had just thanked Dallisa for; her tunic and skirt were much warmer.

She had to go *somewhere*. If she stayed where she was Dallisa might open the door she had just closed, and that would be…well, awkward, at the very least. She began walking, turning south a few blocks later with no particular destination in mind. A spriggan ran across her path, and she kicked idly at it, but didn't connect.

Those things were supposed to be able to talk; maybe she should have asked *it* where she should go.

It was not really a conscious decision, but a few minutes later she realized where she was, and where her feet were taking her – she was on Carpenter Street, and headed for Dulzan's shop.

She had intended to look in on him eventually, of course, but had not planned to do it so soon. She knew that any claim she had ever had on him had expired long ago. She hoped he was all right, and not too lonely – but then even if he hadn't found another woman, he had always had his friends at Tizzi's Tavern. He had the knack of making friends easily, while Sharra had never really made friends at all, at least not since she was a girl, unless you counted her co-workers at the Crooked Mast.

But here she was, scarcely a hundred yards away, and she could not think of anywhere better to go. She looked at the signboards; none of them seemed familiar, but she was accustomed to that now.

Dulzan had never worried much about his signboard; it had been small and elegant, though he had not been able to resist carving some flourishes into the edges. It had simply said DULZAN THE CABINET-MAKER, with no further claims or boasts. She did not see it, and she began to worry that Lador was wrong and Dulzan was gone.

She almost missed it, since she was so focused on finding the little sign she remembered, but at last she looked up and saw it. The new sign was larger than the old, though still not ostentatious, and was painted a deep wine red, with gilded letters and an elaborate gilt border. It read DULZAN & COMPANY, BESPOKE CABINETRY.

She stopped walking and stared. *That* did not sound like Dulzan. "Bespoke cabinetry" – she wished *she* had thought of that slogan, back when they were married! She wondered who had come up with it; it really did *not* sound like something Dulzan would say.

And what did "and company" mean?

She noticed that other pedestrians were starting to glance curiously at her, and she started forward again, walking up to the door.

The door was new, too. Instead of the broad, simple panels and frame of old, this one was beautifully carved and polished, with floral designs surrounding a circular window. She recognized it as unmistakably Dulzan's work.

She opened it and stepped inside, and was once again stunned into immobility.

The shop was two or three times the size it had been when she last saw it; Dulzan had annexed the shop to the north and knocked out the wall, though a row of three polished wooden pillars carved into the shape of graceful young women, hands stretched up to support a ceiling beam, still separated the two spaces.

It was also much cleaner than it had usually been; the floor was spotless. Obviously, the business had thrived.

But the workbench was the same as it had always been, and the display of woods on the wall appeared unchanged. The added space beyond the pillars was taken up with gleaming furniture, tastefully arranged.

Dulzan was nowhere to be seen, but a young man was seated at the workbench, bent over a wooden medallion with a knife in his hand. He did not look up at the sound of the bell, but a young woman was approaching from the newly-added area.

"Can I help you?" she asked.

"I was looking for Dulzan," Sharra said.

"He's not in at the moment. I'm Kirris, his assistant; could I be of service?"

"I don't... I'm not sure," Sharra replied. Perhaps she could be spared the embarrassment of facing her former husband after all – this woman could probably tell her whatever she wanted to know, and would let Dulzan know she was safely back in the city.

She looked at the assistant. She appeared to be in her early twenties, with a face that could be called pleasant, or even pretty, but not beautiful. She wore a white tunic with gold embroidery, a skirt the color of honey, and brown slippers. Her long black hair was tied back out of the way. She gave an impression of competence and friendly interest.

"Were you interested in commissioning a piece?" she asked.

"No." Sharra shook her head. "I'm...an old acquaintance, and I wanted to say hello, and see how he's doing." She looked around the shop. "It appears he's doing well."

Kirris smiled. "He is," she agreed. "He doesn't come into the shop much anymore, but he still oversees everything, and does some of the design work." She gestured toward the workbench. "That's his eldest son, my brother Dabran; he'll be taking over the business if our father ever decides to let it go. There are two journeymen in back who handle most of the assembly work."

"You're Dulzan's daughter?"

"Indeed I am," she said proudly. "As well as his assistant. Who should I tell him was looking for him?"

Sharra hesitated, then swallowed her pride and said, "Sharra the Petty."

Kirris blinked. Her jaw dropped. "Sharra? Sharra the *Petty*? You mean Dad's first wife?"

Sharra was not sure what reaction she had expected, if this woman recognized the name at all, but this wasn't it. "He told you about me?"

"Well, of course he did! He said you were pretty, but... It's really you?"

Sharra nodded.

"He said you had been turned to stone!"

"I was. I was turned back a couple of months ago."

"But that's wonderful!" Kirris exclaimed. "He's felt so guilty! All my life, I've heard him talk about how he blamed himself for what happened to you!"

"It wasn't his fault," Sharra said. "It was my own self-centered stupidity."

Kirris smiled, then grabbed Sharra's arm and called, "Dabran, I have to go somewhere. Watch the shop, or get Obaya to take over."

The man at the workbench grunted an acknowledgment.

Then Kirris was dragging Sharra out the door, chortling, "Oh, this is wonderful! Dad will be so pleased!"

Sharra wished she believed that.

CHAPTER NINETEEN

Sharra had no idea where they were going, but she had enough trouble keeping up with Kirris that she could not quite gather her wits to ask. Kirris dragged her down to the end of Carpenter Street, then half a block along Crosstown Street, past Tizzi's Tavern, out of Crafton and into Southshore, where they marched up an alley wedged between a ropemaker's shop and a glassblower's studio, then up a flight of stairs to a door above the glassblower. She did not bother to knock, but walked in, still dragging Sharra behind her, and called, "Dad! Guess who I found!"

The rooms beyond the door were not elegant, but they had a comfortable, lived-in look, with half a dozen carpets spread across a floor that sagged ever so slightly. Windows at one side gave a view of a courtyard where laundry hung drying, and children were babbling cheerfully as they played.

Most of the furniture was inexpensive and well-worn, but a few pieces stood out – all of them gorgeous wooden cabinets, ranging in size from a small box on a nearby table to a magnificent wardrobe against the far wall. All in all, the place looked nothing at all like the carefully arranged house Sharra and Dulzan had had in Brightside.

"Kirris?" a voice called in response, and Sharra heard footsteps.

Remembering what had become of Lador and Dallisa, Sharra dreaded what she was going to see. Dulzan had been so handsome, but that was thirty years ago...

But then he stepped out of the next room, and he was older, his hair and beard were white, but he was still handsome. He had not gotten fat; he had not gone bald. He stood straight, and his broad shoulders did not sag. His face was wrinkled, but they were the lines of someone who smiled often.

A woman followed behind him, but before Sharra could get a good look at her Dulzan exclaimed, "Sharra! You're alive!"

"So are you!"

He laughed at that – a sound she had not heard in a very, very long time. She could not remember that laughter since the first year or two of their marriage. Before she could say anything more he strode up and embraced her.

Sharra had no idea how best to react; she returned the embrace, but only gently.

At last Dulzan released her. "So Lador finally came up with the money?" he said. "He didn't tell me! I had offered to help if he got close."

"No, it wasn't Lador," she said. "Poldrian never did get his money. Another wizard saved me."

"Really? I'm glad. And you're still so young!"

She started to say, "Statues don't age," but cut herself off before she got the first word out.

"You met Kirris?" Dulzan asked.

Sharra nodded. "I went to your shop."

"She was looking for you," Kirris said.

"She said you…you were worried about me," Sharra said, almost making it a question.

"I was! I always was, all these years. But there wasn't anything I could do; I didn't have that much money to spare after I gave you all my savings. And I was so busy with Marai and the children."

"Marai?"

Dulzan turned, and the woman stepped up beside him.

She was plump – not really fat, but plump, with a round face and large dark eyes. She was clearly a decade or so younger than Dulzan; her hair was still dark. She barely came up to Dulzan's shoulder.

"Sharra," Dulzan said, "this is my wife, Marai of Southshore. Marai, this is Sharra – I've told you about her."

"I'm pleased to see you," Sharra said, with a bow.

"Hello," Marai said, uncertainly.

"I don't think we ever met," Sharra said. "Did we?"

Marai shook her head.

"No, I didn't meet Marai until two or three years after you were enchanted," Dulzan agreed. "And you met Kirris, obviously – what about Dabran?"

"I saw him, but we didn't speak," Sharra said. "He was busy."

Dulzan laughed again. "That sounds like Dabran. The other three are all out somewhere – I'm not sure where. They should be back for supper, if you want to wait."

"I don't…" Sharra began, astonished by the realization that Dulzan had not just one or two, but *five* children.

"Oh, you must stay for supper!" Marai said. "If you don't have other plans, I mean. It won't be any trouble feeding one more."

Sharra hesitated, and glanced at Dulzan; she could not read his expression, but he did not seem to oppose the idea.

She knew that when she had been Dulzan's wife she would never, ever have invited another woman and potential rival to dinner. Clearly, Marai was a very different person – and that was good. That was what Dulzan needed. She felt tears starting to well up; she had wasted twenty years of Dulzan's life, and her own, trying to make him into something else, when this was what he had wanted all along. She had refused to see it, but once she was out of the way he had found it. He was *so much happier* now! In just the few minutes she had been there, she had seen it.

As for supper, it wasn't as if she had anywhere else to go, or any way to pay for her own meal.

"All right," she said.

"Wonderful!" Kirris exclaimed. "You can tell us about all the good times you had with Dad."

Sharra did not think that was a tactful thing to say in front of Marai, her own mother, but what she said was, "No, I don't think so. There really weren't any."

Dulzan started to object, then stopped. He frowned. "No, there weren't, were there?"

"There were times *I* enjoyed, when I got to show off, and I think you had some good times with your friends when I wasn't around, but there were never times *both* of us enjoyed. That's why you left," Sharra said. "You should have done it sooner."

"I…didn't want to hurt you."

"Which was very sweet of you."

"You didn't think so at the time."

"I've had thirty years to think about it. Thirty years to do nothing *but* think." She shook her head. "I was a terrible wife. I was a terrible *person*. But I'm trying to be better now."

"Thirty years?" a voice said behind her. "You don't look thirty!"

Sharra turned to find a girl in her mid-teens standing in the doorway behind her. "I'm older than I look," she said. "Hello; I'm Sharra." She did not provide an epithet.

"I'm Linnis the Stealthy," the girl said.

"She's always been good at sneaking up on people," Marai said, before Sharra could comment.

"You're really pretty," Linnis said. "And you really don't look thirty. You look younger than Kirris, and she's only twenty-three."

"I bought a youth spell."

"*Hai*! Really?"

"Really," Sharra said.

"She did," Dulzan confirmed. "I knew her before."

"You...oh, wait. Sharra? Are you *that* Sharra?"

"I am," she admitted. "Sharra the Petty."

"So then you must be...almost as old as Dad?"

"Almost. I'm sixty-nine." It felt very odd to finally say that aloud, especially as she caught a glimpse of herself in a mirror that hung beside the door. She still looked eighteen or nineteen.

Linnis sucked in her breath in an astonished gasp.

"But you aren't really, are you?" Dulzan said. "You were turned to stone; that time doesn't really count."

"Dulzan," Sharra said gently, "I was conscious even as a statue. I spent thirty years blind and unable to move or feel anything, but I could think and I could hear. It counts."

"How horrible!" Marai exclaimed.

"It was," Sharra agreed.

For a moment the room was silent. "I didn't realize," Dulzan murmured at last.

"Would it have mattered if you did?"

"It might. I might have tried harder to raise the money you owed that wizard."

"Why? It wasn't your fault; you already gave me far more money than I deserved. You should have had that gold for your family."

"But...thirty years!"

Sharra looked at Kirris and Linnis. She thought about saying something about how he had spent that time raising his children, but in the end just said, "It's over now. I'm fine."

"Where are you staying?"

"Well, actually, I hadn't found a place yet..."

"Then you'll stay here!" Marai said.

"Oh, I couldn't..."

"Of course you can! You'll have to share a room with Kirris, but there's enough space."

"You'll have time to tell us all about your adventures!" Kirris said.

"Standing in a corner for thirty years isn't much of an adventure."

"We still want to hear about it!" Linnis said.

Sharra smiled at her. "And you'll have to tell *me* everything that I've missed!" Then she looked at Dulzan. "But I don't want to be any trouble. If it would be awkward to have your ex-wife around, I can find somewhere else."

"If Marai doesn't mind, *I* don't," Dulzan said. "As long as you remember we aren't married, and don't start nagging me."

Linnis giggled.

In the end, Sharra stayed with Dulzan's family for a sixnight.

At dinner the first night, as they ate a meal of stew and crusty bread, she told the entire tale of her giving everything she had to buy the youth spell, and then being turned to stone when it wasn't enough. She did her best to describe what it was like to have no senses but hearing. She explained how her nephew Lador had taken charge of the attempt to rescue her, but had failed miserably and sold her to Lord Landessin.

The older girls, Kirris and Linnis, were fascinated; the youngest, Shallis, and the younger boy, Dunrel, liked some parts but were obviously bored by others. Dabran, the eldest, had never come back from the shop; Dulzan assured Sharra that that was not at all unusual, and was nothng to worry about. He was undoubtedly focused on a piece of work, and would come home either when it was done, or when the lamps ran out of oil – or he might sleep in the back of the shop; there was still a cot there. Dabran was twenty-five and could take care of himself.

Sharra told the part of the family that was still listening about what she had heard in those long years standing in the corner of the entry hall, how she had heard life going on around her while she could do nothing to participate, and how she had more than enough time to think about her life, and what she had done wrong. Dunrel and Shallis ignored this part, and instead started poking one another until Dulzan firmly told them to behave.

And finally, she described how Morvash of the Shadows had set out to save all the petrified people in Lord Landessin's collection, and had succeeded after months of effort – and how she had stupidly refused his offer of help because she was so eager to get home to her own city.

"…and when I went back he was gone," she said. "The front door of the house was broken, and the place was empty. A demon had smashed its way in."

At the mention of a demon Shallis began paying attention again. The three girls at the table, Kirris, Linnis, and Shallis, looked at one another. "Was that *Tarker*?" Shallis asked.

"Who?" Sharra asked, startled.

"Tarker the Unrelenting," Kirris said. "It's a demon that's stuck in our world until it finishes killing this gigantic stone dragon. Last month it broke off a piece and brought it to a place near the overlord's palace where wizards' spells don't work, and since it had been wizardry that brought the dragon to life, the broken-off piece died when it got there."

"We didn't see it," Shallis said.

"But we heard about it from people who were there," Linnis said.

"They say that Tarker will be bringing the rest of the dragon there, one piece at a time, until it's all gone," Kirris said. "I think the next piece should be coming soon; maybe we can arrange to watch, though they say there isn't much to see, just a demon carrying a big rock."

"The overlord's men broke up the first rock, and sold the pieces as souvenirs," Linnis said. "My friend Helmira has one." She turned up an empty palm. "It just looks like a rock."

"Why do you think it might be the same demon?" Sharra asked.

"Well, there are stories about where the demon came from, and where the dragon came from," Kirris explained. "And one story was that the dragon was brought to life by a wizard who had practiced for it by turning statues into people, so we thought maybe that was your Morvash, and you were one of the people he practiced on, and the demon that's trying to kill the dragon had tried to kill *you*…"

"No, there were *two* wizards," Linnis interrupted.

"There *were* two wizards," Sharra confirmed, reaching for another chunk of bread. "Morvash and that tall thin one who spoke some other language. I'm guessing *he* was the one who brought the dragon to life, if either of them did it; he seemed much more powerful than Morvash."

"Well, anyway, wizards were bringing stone to life and a demon was involved both times," Kirris said. "It's not unreasonable to think it might be the same demon."

"I suppose not," Sharra agreed.

"Go on and tell us the rest!" Shallis demanded. "How did you get back to the Sands?"

"Oh, I think I've talked enough for now," Sharra said. "Suppose *you* tell *me* what's happened while I was away."

The two older girls exchanged glances.

"Well, we were born," Linnis said.

"I noticed that," Sharra said. "Marai, why don't you tell me how you met Dulzan?"

"What? Oh, that's not…"

"Go on, Mama, it's a cute story!" Kirris exclaimed.

"I'll tell it," Dulzan said. "And you've heard it before, you four, so if you want to leave you may."

Dunrel left; the three girls stayed.

After Sharra was petrified, Dulzan had gone about his life, spending his days at the shop and his evenings at Tizzi's Tavern, and occasionally going home with someone female, but not becoming particularly attached to anyone – nor they to him.

But on one such occasion a widow had been interested in commissioning a chest of drawers, and in Dulzan's attempts to measure the space it was intended to fit he had bumped against an iron lampstand, which had toppled and set off a chain reaction that resulted in a hole in the wall separating the widow's apartment from an adjoining one.

Marai's mother had lived on the other side of that hole, and one thing had led to another…

By the time the story was over dinner was long since finished. Shallis had departed, while Marai, Dulzan, and Kirris were cleaning up.

CHAPTER TWENTY

During her stay with Dulzan's family Sharra finished telling her hosts the details of her adventures, and in exchange learned about how the Empress Tabaea had taken over the city, how the now-powerless warlocks had returned from Aldagmor, how magnificent old Ederd IV's funeral had been, and much more. She and the family talked at length about the area near the palace where wizardry didn't work; if she had been taken there as a statue, would that have broken the spell and restored her to life, or would it have turned her *entirely* to stone and killed her? So far as any of them knew, it had never been tested – after all, there weren't all that many petrified people around; Lord Landessin had bought most of them long ago and hauled them off to Ethshar of the Spices.

And of course, the magic-stopping spell hadn't existed until after Tabaea was killed, only about ten or twelve years ago, so it couldn't have helped for the first twenty years she spent as a statue.

If Morvash had known about that special place, they speculated, he might have tested it, but the Wizards' Guild had tried to keep it secret – right up until Tarker began dragging pieces of dragon there.

Even if Morvash had known about it, it might not have occurred to him to try it.

In return, Sharra told Dulzan's children what she remembered of some of the major events that happened before they were born, such as the Night of Madness, and the day Helikar the Mage inadvertently unleashed thousands of pink rabbits on the city's streets.

On the second day after her arrival in the city she visited Poldrian's shop. Four spriggans were hanging around outside, and she worried that they might follow her in, but apparently there was a protective spell that prevented them from entering the shop. They simply watched with unhappy expressions as she went in.

Poldrian's old apprentice was long gone, of course, but he had a new one, a boy of no more than fourteen, who was not yet entirely sure of his duties. He seemed very impressed with Sharra's beauty, and she had no trouble talking her way past him into Poldrian's workroom.

The wizard was seated on a stool by a rough wooden table, reading a large book; he had not aged visibly, and in fact she thought he appeared a little younger than she remembered, but after all, as Sharra was well aware, he knew at least one youth spell. He looked up as she entered, and sighed.

"I really need to have a word with that apprentice of mine," he said.

"I'm sorry to bother you," Sharra said. "I just had a question."

"About my fee?"

"You remember me, after all this time?"

"The first person I ever petrified? Of course I do."

"Well, then – about your fee…"

He waved a hand in dismissal. "Forget it," he said. "I don't need the money, I made my point, and even if I *did* turn you back to stone, someone would probably just haul you down to the plaza to see whether that…that dead spot would reverse it."

"Would it?"

"How should *I* know? I haven't tested it. Anyway, I said I'd turn you to stone if you didn't pay me, I did turn you to stone, and that's the end of it. I said I'd turn you back if someone paid me the balance, but obviously someone else beat me to it, so we're done. Go; we're done."

"Thank you!" She bowed quickly, and hurried out before he could change his mind.

On the third day after her return Sharra finally got up the courage to visit Nerra and their mother. She approached warily, and knocked, just once.

Nerra's voice – familiar, but changed by age – called, "Who is it?"

"Sharra."

There was a clatter of footsteps; then Nerra flung the door open and immediately threw her arms around her sister in a powerful hug.

That was a pleasant surprise; after the reception she had from Dallisa, she had not anticipated much of a welcome from her other sister. Nerra, too, had aged normally through the entire thirty years;

her hair was white and thinning, and her face was lined, but her breath against Sharra's cheek was warm and her hands were steady.

"We were worried about you!" Nerra said, releasing her hold. "When Lador told us you were back we expected you to come here right away, and then you never came!"

"I...was visiting friends," Sharra said.

"Friends?" Nerra blinked.

Sharra did not explain; she just nodded.

"Well, it's amazing to see you after so long! I was so happy to hear that the spell had been broken and you were all right. And you still look so young, just like the statue – though you're in more sensible clothes, I see."

"I sold the dress," Sharra said.

"That was probably for the best. Come in!"

"I needed the money," she said as she stepped into the apartment. "Did I tell Dallisa I sold it? I meant to. It was so kind of her to make it."

"You told her. Lador said you were stranded in Ethshar of the Spices?"

"Yes. It's a long story. Is Mama here? Lador said she was living with you."

"Oh, of course she's here! She doesn't go out much. I'll see if she's awake." Nerra headed into another room; Sharra followed, and her sister did not object.

Kirsha was sitting in a chair by the window, her head sunk forward in a doze. "Mama?" Nerra called.

Sharra felt tears starting at the sight of her mother, shrunken and wrinkled, raising her head as if that simple movement required effort and concentration. "Mama?" she said. "It's me. I've come back."

Kirsha turned to look at her, and her face slowly broke into a smile. "Sharra?" she said, her voice brittle with age. "Where have you *been*?"

Sharra was not sure just how aware her mother was. Was she asking where Sharra had been for the last three days, or for the last thirty years? "Staying with friends, Mama," she said.

That seemed to satisfy Kirsha. "Come give me a hug!" she said.

Sharra did not need to be asked twice; she hurried and knelt by the chair, and wrapped her mother in her arms, her head on the old woman's shoulder.

Sharra stayed for most of the afternoon, and quickly saw that sometimes Kirsha knew what was going on, and sometimes she slipped back into the past. Once she asked Sharra how the plans for her wedding to Dulzan were going, and when Sharra said it had been cancelled she seemed upset for a few minutes, but then remembered.

"Oh, he left you, didn't he?"

"Yes, Mama. He found someone else, someone better for him. Her name is Marai, and he's happy with her."

"But what about *you*?"

"I'm still young, Mama," she said, and she realized that physically, she still was. She had been telling everyone she was older than she looked, and in a way she always would be, but she didn't *need* to be older anymore as far as others were concerned. "I'll find someone else."

That confused her. "You're…young?"

"Look at me, Mama. I'll be fine."

Kirsha looked up at her, and then over at Nerra, who was obviously *not* young. "I don't understand."

"It's magic, Mama. A wizard did it."

"A wizard? Why were you fooling around with wizards?"

"It was a mistake, Mama. I won't do it again."

"That's good. Wizards are dangerous." With that, her head started to fall forward, but she caught herself.

"Do you need to rest, Mama?" Nerra asked.

"That would be nice."

"Then we'll let you rest." She beckoned to Sharra.

Reluctantly, Sharra pulled away. "Sleep well, Mama," she said. "I love you."

She and Nerra left their mother asleep in the sunlight and went into the other room.

It was the following day when Lador found her and presented her with a bag of gold. "Nine rounds," he said. "That's all Mother would give me, but it should be enough to make a new start."

"It will," Sharra agreed, accepting the money.

She had been asking around; she did not want to impose on Dulzan any longer than necessary. She had found a pleasant little room on the third floor above a dressmaker's shop that she thought might suit her, but she hadn't had any way to pay the rent.

Now she did.

She took two days to furnish the room, and then moved in, with Kirris helping.

It was an odd thing, but during her stay with Dulzan she had spent progressively less and less time with Dulzan himself, or even with Marai, and more and more with Kirris, and to a lesser extent with Linnis. To all appearances she fell between them in age, and she was growing steadily more comfortable with that apparent age. Dulzan had been part of her *old* life, the life she had been so desperate to return to, but she had finally realized that that life was gone, irretrievably lost. She needed to build a *new* one.

And while she might not have a family to support her in the usual ways, she had an advantage over any other young woman of eighteen or nineteen – she knew many mistakes to avoid.

She knew she should have finished her apprenticeship, rather than throwing it away to marry Dulzan, and she thought she might be able to talk a weaver into taking her on to fix that mistake. Explaining that she had been enchanted, so her old master was no longer available, without mentioning that she had quit long before being enchanted – that would be a deceit, but she thought it would be a forgivable one.

Or if all else failed, she could apprentice herself to Lador. He owed her that much.

She realized now that her appearance and her status were not the most important things in the World.

She had seen how happy, how *comfortable*, Dulzan was in his new marriage, and she hoped she might find something like that someday. She wished she hadn't prevented him from finding his happiness sooner; maybe if she hadn't made those regular visits to Mother Maffi she and Dulzan could have made a loving family, but that possibility was long past now.

But there were many more possibilities ahead. After all, she was still young.

EPILOGUE

Sharra and Kirris were standing on Circle Street, near where Quarter Street emptied into the plaza, waiting for Tarker the Unrelenting to bring the next chunk of the stone dragon to be destroyed. They had been chattering about the young man Kirris had met the day before at her father's shop, and about the young man Sharra had met a few days earlier at Grandgate Market, when Sharra noticed someone staring at them. She stopped talking and looked at the woman.

She looked familiar.

When she saw that Sharra had noticed her, the woman came over, and despite her age Sharra recognized her. This was Lady Ramassa, one of the people that Sharra had tried so very, very hard to impress during her marriage to Dulzan.

"Excuse me," Ramassa said. "It's been a long time, but aren't you Sharra the…the Charming?"

Sharra smiled. "No," she said. "I'm Sharra the Younger."